He was looking at her body. Dark eyes were hidden beneath those spiky black lashes as they gazed over a smooth white shoulder then dipped lower to the rounded slopes of her breasts. He wanted to touch her.

"No," she breathed in shaky rejection, and made a clumsy grab at the slipping duvet.

Her denial brought his lashes up. Black heat shot up toward her and held her trapped in a dark mesh. The duvet remained where it was, lying in a soft squashy heap on her lap, and the sting of desire leapt through her blood, tripping sensual switches as it went.

He knew—he knew. Everything about him was turning dark on the knowledge. Dark eyes, dark heart, a searing dark ardor that coiled itself around the both of them. Nothing about him was light anymore, nothing gentle or soft. He wanted her, but didn't want to want her. She returned the resentful feeling.

Michelle Reid

THE SALVATORE MARRIAGE

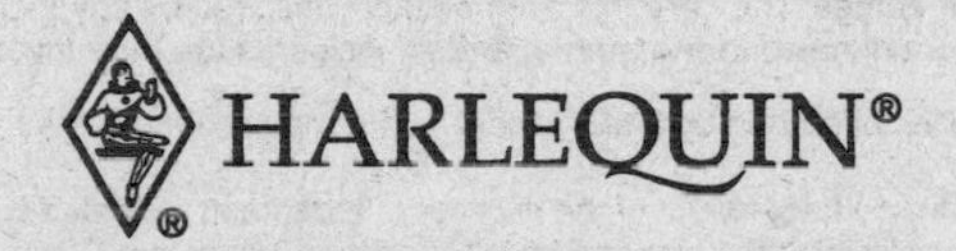

TORONTO • NEW YORK • LONDON
AMSTERDAM • PARIS • SYDNEY • HAMBURG
STOCKHOLM • ATHENS • TOKYO • MILAN • MADRID
PRAGUE • WARSAW • BUDAPEST • AUCKLAND

ISBN 0-373-12362-0

THE SALVATORE MARRIAGE

First North American Publication 2003.

This edition published by arrangement with Harlequin Books S.A.

Visit us at www.eHarlequin.com

Printed in U.S.A.

CHAPTER ONE

THE storm raging outside was killing the signal. Shannon uttered a soft, tense little curse as trembling fingers reset her cell-phone then hit 'redial' before pushing the phone back to her ear.

Fear was crawling over her skin like a swarm of invading spiders. She couldn't stop shivering—or was she trembling? She didn't know, didn't care, she just needed—*needed* to make this connection.

'Come on...' she prayed with teeth-gritting tension when still nothing happened.

Five minutes ago she had been dashing from a taxi to her apartment block with no other concern than to get out of the driving rain. She'd had a hell of a day from the moment she'd overslept that morning. In her haste to catch her flight to Paris, she'd rushed out of her flat forgetting to pick up her cell-phone as she left and had felt lost without it all day.

On top of that, her meeting had not been worth the time she had wasted on it. Temperamental supermodels and gifted graphic designers just did not mix, she'd discovered, especially when the supermodel in question took one look at the graphic designer's slender, long-legged figure and regarded her as an instant threat. Why the heck the idiot had conjured up the idea that a five-foot-eight redhead could compete with a six-foot-tall sylph-slim blonde with cheekbones to die for was anyone's guess. But all hope that the model was going to let Shannon design her self-promoting website went out of the window then and there.

Since then Shannon had flown back to London through the worst weather imaginable, struggled to get a taxi, then had got soaked getting from it to here. The first thing she saw on stepping through her front door was her cell-phone lying on the hall table, innocently telling her that she'd received a dozen missed calls—most of which were from her business partner Joshua demanding to know why the hell she wasn't answering her phone.

But it was another message awaiting her that had sent her mind into a complete meltdown. 'Shannon,' it said. 'Call me back on this number as soon as you can. There has been an—accident.'

An accident— Her throat closed on her effort to swallow. The relater of the message had not left his name but through the static his deep, smooth, accented voice had been familiar enough to put her into this state of raw panic. She guessed that the call was from her sister's husband Angelo—and if Angelo had left such a message then it could only be because the accident involved Keira.

'Damn,' she muttered when still nothing happened, and was hitting redial again when the doorbell gave a short, sharp ring.

Distracted, she turned to walk down the hallway, barely noticing that she had to step over the bag she'd left dumped in the middle of the floor as she made her way to the front door. A set of harried fingers made a wild scrape through the silk straight weight of her rain-dampened hair before continuing on to grasp the door latch. The phone still wasn't connecting. She tugged the door open, too preoccupied to wonder who might be standing on the other side of it so it came as a shock—a cold, hard, breath catching shock to find the last person on earth she ever expected to see standing there.

He stood over six feet two inches tall and was wearing a long black overcoat. The width of his shoulders almost spanned the doorway. For a few awful moments Shannon actually felt dizzy enough to clutch at the door while he stood there filling the opening like some dark, chilling force.

'Luca.' Dear God, she thought as her lips framed his name on a stunned whisper.

He didn't utter a single word but just reached out with a hand to ease the phone from her numbed fingers, then began ushering her backwards by the economical means of taking a step forwards.

Her breath feathered against her ribcage, the fact that she wasn't yelling at him to get the hell away from her said a lot about her state of near complete shutdown—though she did manage to register that both of them moved without touching anywhere. Like a dance between two opposing magnets, they made the manoeuvre into her hall without breaching each other's defensive space until she was standing with her back pressed against a wall, eyes wide and fixed unblinkingly on him as he turned his back on her and in grim, grim silence closed the door.

The size of her hall suddenly shrank to nothing, she felt strange suddenly, as if she too were shrinking into herself in an effort to get away from what she was being faced with here.

This man, this larger-than-life figurehead of the vast Salvatore empire. Luca Salvatore, of Florence, a man of power and of unrivalled passion. Ex-lover to Shannon Gilbraith, woman of sin and sister to his brother's wife.

He was also the man she had been going to marry. The man she had lived with like a wife for six wonderful months before it had all come crashing in. She'd loved him passionately; now she could barely have him look at her without feeling her heart wither in his presence.

He turned slowly to face her, shedding raindrops from his wide shoulders as he did so and filling the confined space with the smell of cold air and rain on wool. His long lashed gaze flicked her a glance then slid away to take in the bag dumped on the floor.

'You've been away,' he murmured levelly. His English was perfect, smooth and deep with the kind of accent that played across her senses like the brush of a lover's—

Don't go there, she told herself. 'P-Paris,' she said.

He nodded his dark head as if she'd just confirmed something for him, though for the life of her she couldn't work out what. She was shaking all over, racked by too many confusing conflicts, aware that she should be thinking about her sister but able to think only about him.

Keira... Her throat convulsed on a wave of anguish, the flat of her palms pressed into the wall. Lifting anxious blue eyes to the hard, tight lines of his profile, she parted her lips to demand he tell her what had happened to Keira, but Luca spoke first.

'Are we alone here?' he questioned, and when she just gaped at him, unable to believe he had dared to ask that question, he decided to find out for himself. Stepping over her bag, he began opening doors.

Shock was replaced by burning dismay when she realised what he was doing. Two years ago Luca had arrived at his apartment in Florence to find her making a hurried attempt to cover up the evidence of what she had been doing while he'd been out of the way. What followed had been a gruesome demonstration of what came to pass when you played a Salvatore for a fool.

That time he had dragged her from room to room with him as he'd checked all the places in which she could have hidden a lover. This time he was prepared to make the search on his own—not that he had any right to do so.

'You bastard,' she breathed, and found the strength to push herself away from the wall and walk on trembling legs into her sitting room.

She hadn't had a chance to come in here, she realised,

staring blankly into the room's chilly darkness that was softened only by the halogen glow from an outside street lamp filtering in through the window. It was automatic to reach for the nearest switch and flood the room with proper light—automatic to cross to the window to tug the cream curtains over the rain-soaked glass.

When she turned she found him standing in the doorway staring at her through narrowed dark brown, gold-flecked eyes set in a face that wore the proud stamp of his Florentine lineage. He was handsome but hard; handsome but cold; forge a statue in his image and you would have yourself a reflection of a modern-day god.

But this man was no god, she reminded herself quickly. He might have the face and the body of one, might possess the kind of power and arrogance the old gods liked to wield, but inside he was as mortal as anyone. Flawed and fickle, she concluded as she waited for the shock to ease so that the old bitter emotions could come flooding in.

Emotions like pain and anger, and the miserable ache of a love cruelly ripped away from her—a passionately professed, returned love that she'd learned the hard way had never gone more than skin-deep for him.

It didn't happen. Standing here white-faced and tensed in readiness for it all to surge up and grab her, Shannon discovered that she continued to feel absolutely nothing, not even a slight twinge of that old sense of desperation with which mere thoughts of him used to fill her. Those eyes that used to turn her heart inside out were leaving her cold now, as did the slender mouth that used to act like a magnet to her own hungry lips. The slashing high cheek-bones, the dark golden skin, the magnificent body hidden beneath the heavy coat; she used to worship all of them with every touch, every breath or sensual homage she could find. The man in his whole god-like entirety was doing nothing for her any more.

It came as such a relief, because it had to mean that she was over him.

Over him at last and for ever.

'Satisfied with your search?' she asked with acid-tipped sarcasm. 'Or would you like to check behind the curtains too?'

There was a hint of a frown before he acknowledged the comment with a small grimace.

'No,' was all he said and he shifted his gaze to take in the décor with its soft pastel shades and neat modern furniture that was such a contrast to the antique luxury he'd furnished his own home with. Her small twin sofas were covered with cream linen, her floor was of pale polished wood. His floors displayed priceless rugs thrown over intricate inlaid wood parquetry and his sofas were made of rich brown leather that were big and deep enough to stretch out upon two at a time to canoodle and kiss in exquisite—

Once again she was forced to bring her wandering thoughts up short. Why recall all of that when it no longer meant anything? she asked herself crossly, and moved across the room to flick another switch, which sent flames leaping up over designer logs resting on a bed of pale pebbles in her open hearth.

This time when she turned she found that his attention had switched back to her again, his hooded gaze moving over her pencil-slim skirt with its natty little kick pleat at the back, which gave her long legs a rather sexy shape. Did he like her legs? Of course he liked her legs; he used to worship them with his hands and his mouth and the teasing lick from his tongue as it trailed upwards on its way to—

Oh, stop it! she told herself. He looked up suddenly, as if she'd said the words out loud. Their eyes connected. Tension erupted to rush screaming round the room on the back of a mutual, intimate knowledge that would never go away no matter how much they both might want it to.

They'd been lovers, gorgeous, greedy, sensually indulgent lovers. They knew every inch of each other, what made the other sigh with pleasure and what would send them toppling over the edge. But those thoughts did not belong here—*he* didn't belong here!

Say something, damn you! she wanted to scream at him. But he'd always been good at using silence to whittle down people's nerves, and he continued to stand there looking at her as if he was waiting for *her* to say something. Say what? she wondered. Was he expecting her to invite him to sit down?

The phrase about burning in hell first whipped through her head.

Maybe he heard it. Maybe he was still able to tune himself in to what was going on inside her head because the black silk lashes flickered slightly as he shifted his gaze yet again and fixed it on something over her right shoulder.

Shannon didn't need to look to know what it was that had now caught his attention. It had to be the framed wedding photograph standing alone on a shelf that showed the sweet face of her sister Keira smiling adoringly up at his handsome brother Angelo.

Behind the blissful couple and fortunately out of focus stood Luca, playing the dauntingly sophisticated best man to the groom and herself as the young and self-conscious chief bridesmaid. Luca had been all of twenty-eight years old to her own meagre eighteen at the time, but they'd enjoyed each other's company that day.

Odd, she thought, that she should remember that now when there were so many bad things about Luca she could be remembering instead.

'I think it might be best if you sit down.'

Muscles all over her body jerked suddenly, bringing her chin up sharply as her senses leapt in alarm. When someone told you to sit down it could only mean they were about to tell you something that was guaranteed to take the legs from under you, and the only way this man could do that to her was by bringing her bad news about—

'What's wrong with Keira?' she shot at him sharply.

A hand came out; long-fingered and lean, it indicated to one of the sofas. 'When you sit down,' he countered, then watched calmly as if he was expecting it as she sparked like a firework.

'Oh, stop being so bloody sensitive to my feelings, Luca, and tell me what's happened to my sister!' she cried. 'All I got was some static-splashed message telling me that there had been an accident and would I ring a stupid mobile phone number that did not exist!'

'It exists,' he murmured.

And like a lightning strike Shannon suddenly realised what a terrible—terrible—mistake she had made. 'It was your mobile number, wasn't it?' she bit out accusingly, struggling to believe that she could *ever* have mistaken the deep, terse tones of his voice for the warmer tones of his brother Angelo. 'Poor Luca,' she mocked with sudden bitterness, 'being forced to give the wicked witch his new number and risk a second flood of unwanted calls.'

His half-grimace acknowledged her right to toss that remark at him. Two years ago she'd tried every which way she could use to get him to talk to her. She'd called him on his cell-phone night and day until suddenly the number had been no longer obtainable. He'd cut off her main source of contact—just as she'd been ruthlessly cut off from everything else that had been important to her.

'Just speak, damn you,' she prompted huskily.

With a grim pressing-together of his lips, Luca looked ready to continue holding out until she sat down. Then she saw his eyes make a flickering inventory of the way she was standing there, fine-boned and slender enough that the tremors now shaking her body almost forced her down. Stubbornness held her upright; stubbornness and a defiance that had always been one of her most besetting sins in his eyes—though not her worst sin.

Then—no, she slammed a door shut on that kind of thinking. Stop going there! she told herself angrily. Don't think about anything. Don't even bother to notice the way he's looking at you again with a contempt he believes you deserve. So he hates and despises you. Let him, she invited. I don't care—I don't.

He moved then, and on a thick, inner quiver of fear she saw his expression alter from hard to grave. His eyes flicked away. He heaved in a deep breath. The fine hairs on her body started to tingle as he parted his mouth to speak.

Then the words came. 'There has been an accident—a car crash this morning,' he told her. 'People are hurt—badly hurt,' he then extended grimly.

'Keira—?' Her sister's name arrived as a fragile whisper.

'Yes.' He nodded. 'And I need you to be strong here, Shannon,' he warned then, 'because the prognosis is not good and we need to— Oh, hell—you mad, stubborn *idiota*!'

Shannon didn't know she'd swayed until his hands arrived hard on her shoulders and forcibly manoeuvred her into the nearest sofa. She landed with a bump, eyes wide and staring.

'Why can you *never* take good advice when it is offered to you?' he ground out as he came down on his haunches and took a strong grasp on her ice-cold hands. 'It was a simple request—a *wise* request. You almost collapsed as I knew you would. You are your own worst enemy, do you know that? I cannot believe you are still such a—'

She tugged her hands free. The action silenced his angry tongue, snapped his lips together and tightened the muscles in his face. In the new silence that developed Shannon struggled to get a hold of what was trampling through her. Her heart was palpitating wildly, her breathing reduced to tight and shallow catches of air. Keira was the only person left in this world that she truly cared about.

Keira, her beautiful Keira, whom everyone loved and wanted a piece of.

'Tell me what happened,' she whispered unevenly.

His mouth had developed a white ring of tension around it. She had to look away because she couldn't bear to see him while he said what he had to say. 'They were in the fast lane on the main *autostradale* into Florence when they ran into a heavy downpour of rain,' he explained. 'An articulated lorry skidded on the wet surface. It cricco-accoltellato—jackknifed directly in front of them, swerving right across the road. They did not stand a chance,' he uttered in a voice like thick gravel. 'With no room or time to take avoiding action they hit head-on and—'

The words stopped when he was forced to swallow. Silence returned, crawling all over the two of them while Shannon sat staring over the top of Luca's dark head as the whole wretched thing played itself like a macabre action movie in front of her eyes.

'Is she—?'

'No,' he cut in quickly—roughly.

Relief feathered through her, then she tensed again as the next dreaded thought flipped into her head.

'They. You said *they*,' she prompted shakily, and looked at him then, really looked at him and saw for the first time the strain etched into the fabric of his lean, hard features—and the pain burning in the deep, dark depths of his eyes. Realisation dawned, the muscles in her own face began to collapse, tears of a desperate, desperate understanding flooding into her eyes.

'Oh, no, Luca—no,' she choked out unevenly. 'Please,' she begged, 'not Angelo…'

But the answer she wanted to hear didn't come, and as a

set of her cold fingers jerked up to cover her trembling mouth Luca muttered something thick in Italian, then lowered his head to bury his face in his hands.

Dark mists of shock and grief wrapped around them. For what could have been an age Shannon couldn't move or think or even feel. Angelo and Keira—Keira and Angelo—the two precious names spun in her head on an ever dizzying spiral while the rain lashed wildly at the window and Luca remained squatting in front of her with his face covered and his wide shoulders taut as he fought his own battle with shock and grief.

Luca and his brother were close. They worked together, played together, laughed and talked together all the time. To think of one without thinking about the other was—

'Oh Luca…' Lifting her hand with its trembling fingers, Shannon gently touched them to his rain-dampened hair. 'I'm so s—'

It came without warning. At the first light brush of her fingers he was thrusting away from her with a violence that left her stunned and shaken as he climbed to his feet, turned his back on her and strode away several paces to then stand still and rigid while he fought a battle with his moment of complete collapse.

When he turned to face her he was back in control again, or as controlled as a man could be who'd just lost the brother he loved. Shannon hadn't moved, and as his gaze lashed over her she saw the ice, the cold hatred, and knew what he was thinking. He was thinking he did not deserve to lose his brother and she did not deserve to have her sister still.

Yes, she thought, he hated her enough to think like that.

Bitterness returned, and with it came a welcome sense of foggy calmness. Shannon climbed to her feet, wished with all her aching heart that she could just walk away from him, but there were still things she needed to know.

'Y-you said the prognosis for Keira isn't good,' she prompted, feeling the shake in her voice as well as in the fingers she used to smooth down the rucked fabric of her slender skirt. 'Why isn't it good?'

The tense shape of his mouth slackened slightly as he parted his lips to speak. 'Her injuries were extensive. She had to be cut out of the car—'

Shannon flinched and lowered her eyes from him, painfully aware that the *they* had now changed to *she*. Did that mean that Angelo had been beyond help? She didn't ask, didn't dare, didn't think she could cope with the answer.

'By the time they freed her, Keira had lost a lot of blood,' Luca continued in a low voice like rough sandpaper. 'Thankfully she was unconscious throughout so was aware of—nothing…'

The *nothing* broke into uneven fragments, and as her heavy lungs tried their best to breathe for her Shannon wondered if Angelo had been aware of nothing.

Angelo. An ache hit low in her stomach. Never to see his lazy grin again or the teasing gleam in his beautiful eyes—'Oh,' she choked and her legs went hollow, forcing her to sit down again and cover her face with her hands.

'There were problems,' Luca pushed on relentlessly, obviously deciding to get the whole wretched thing said now he had begun. 'Some of which the doctors could fix, some they—could not…'

It was during this next thick pause Luca allowed to develop—presumably to give her time to absorb what he'd said—Shannon suddenly remembered something she should not have forgotten: there was still yet another being involved in this awful tragedy.

A sudden rush of nausea forced her to swallow thickly. Sliding her hand away from her face, she looked up at Luca, her eyes dark and haunted. 'Oh, God, Luca,' she whispered frailly. 'What about the baby?'

Her sister was seven and a half months pregnant—the longest period Keira had managed to carry a baby, one of her many, many attempts to bear Angelo a child. His eyelashes flickered, lowering over dark brown irises to hide his own feelings about what he was about to say. 'They had to do a Caesarean section,' he informed her briefly. 'Keira was haemorrhaging badly and it became a matter of urgency that they deliver the baby as quickly as they could—'

The abruptly spoken words came to a stop again. It seemed that he could only give information in short bursts before he had to pause to gather himself. It was all so dark and utterly wretched, shock piling upon shock upon horror and grief and blood-curdling dread.

'And…?' It took a tight clutching at her courage to prompt him to continue.

'A girl,' he announced. 'She is quite small and needs the aid of an incubator to breathe, but otherwise the doctors assure us that she is fully formed and perfectly healthy. It—it is her mama that gives grave cause for concern. Keira now lies in a coma and I'm afraid the final outcome does not look good.'

In the cold, dark silence that followed, Shannon knew she was slipping into deep shock. Angelo was dead, her sister was dying, their baby daughter needed help to breathe. It couldn't get any worse.

It could, she discovered. 'I'm sorry,' he said gruffly.

But he wasn't sorry, not for her at any rate. It was too late for him to murmur polite words of sympathy when he'd looked at her the way he'd done a few minutes ago. He resented bitterly the fact that he had lost his beloved brother while she, the undeserving one, could still cling to a small thread of hope.

'Excuse me,' she said thickly, 'but I'm going to be sick,' and, dragging herself up from the sofa, she made a dash for the bathroom.

He didn't follow and Shannon did not expect him to—though he had to hear her retching because she hadn't had time to close the door. But she could feel his presence like a scar on her heaving body because this was a scene they had played before, though under very different circumstances.

And remembering that ugly moment made her feel suddenly very bitter that it had to be him of all people to bring her bad news and then witness this.

Trembling too badly to stand unaided, she sank down on the toilet seat lid and tried to think. She had to plan, she had to deal with Luca on a calm and sane footing, because if she was sure about anything in this sudden dizzying nightmare she had been tossed into, then it was that he would have pre-empted her immediate needs and have had travel arrangements put into place before he had even knocked on her door.

It was the way of the man—of the Salvatore family as a whole. Incisive efficiency under pressure was their trademark. They were rich, they were powerful, they dealt with their enemies in the same way that they dealt with tragedy, by closing ranks and, with shields in place, dealing with the situation as one dynamic force.

All for one, one for all, she mused bleakly. Then she thought about Keira lying in a hospital bed somewhere, and even as the family grieved for Angelo she knew that her sister would still be surrounded by their tight ring of protection. The image should have comforted her but instead she found herself having to make another lurching dive for the washbasin.

Why? Because she was not included. She was the outcast sent into exile for her so-called sins. And the prospect of having to break her way through the Salvatore guard to be with her own sister caused the same nauseating distress that had kept her out of Florence for the last two years.

'Oh, Keira…' she groaned on a sob of anguish. Then she thought of poor Angelo and knew that one constrained sob was not going to be enough, so she switched on the taps and wept with the rush of water drowning out the sound.

Luca wasn't in the sitting room when eventually she went back to face him. The all too familiar scent of him lingered, though, catching at her nostrils and relaying messages to certain senses she did not want disturbed. Strange how she had not picked up on that scent earlier.

Even stranger that she'd dared to tell herself that she was over him.

Well, not any longer, she was forced to accept as she turned to go and find him and spied his overcoat lying across the back of one of the chairs in the old familiar way that brought weak tears springing back to her eyes.

Something had happened to her back there in the bathroom. A door inside her had opened and allowed too many suppressed memories to come flooding out. Memories of love and passion and a promise of perfect happiness turning to dust at her feet. And other memories of a sister she had loved more than anyone. Yet when she'd left Luca she had also turned her back on Keira.

Guilt thudded at her conscience, but it fought with resentment and a deep, deep sense of betrayal that still hurt two years on. There were many ways to break someone's heart for them, she mused bleakly. Luca and Keira both had broken her heart in different ways.

She found him standing in her kitchen by one of the modern white units, his six-foot-two-inch frame dwarfing the room as it did most things—including her more diminutive size. He was in the process of pouring boiling water into her smart glass and steel coffee pot but on hearing her step he turned his dark head. For a brief moment she saw him as she had last seen him two years ago, angry, naked, the natural colour washed out of his skin by disgust and contempt and an appalling knowledge of what he had just done.

Then the image faded and now she saw a tired man living with the strain of grief locked up inside him and a knowledge that life had to go on just as duty must still be done.

He offered her a brief smile before turning away again. 'I thought we both needed this,' he explained levelly, drawing her attention to the freshly made pot of coffee he had prepared. 'I have also made you some toast to help to settle your stomach.'

Following the indication of his dark head she saw a plate sitting on the breakfast counter bearing two slices of lightly toasted wholemeal bread. Her stomach lurched again—not at the thought of receiving anything in its tender state, but because the whole scenario was resurrecting yet more memories of the old times. Times when this wealthy, very sophisticated and utterly spoiled man had surprised her with domestic moments like this.

He owned homes in many prestigious places, owned aeroplanes and helicopters and a beautiful yacht that could take one's breath away. He ran a huge multinational finance company that employed thousands of people right across the globe but he didn't like servants intruding on his privacy, suffered their services as a necessity in his busy life so long as they did their work when he wasn't there. He could cook, he could clean and he made the best cup of coffee she had ever tasted.

But here in her kitchen—acting as if he actually cared about her well-being?

Fresh bitterness welled at his damned hypocrisy. 'I'd rather be going,' she replied with as much composure as she could muster. 'That is presuming you've made arrangements for me to travel to Florence?'

'Of course,' he confirmed. 'But we do not have to leave for another hour. My plane needs to refuel and perform the usual checks then wait for a vacant slot before it can take off again.'

'You mean you've flown here from Florence—today?' Shannon was stunned and it showed in the stifled gasp she released.

'Someone had to break the news to you.' The way he shrugged a broad shoulder was meant to convey indifference to the task but they both knew it was a lie. His brother had just died in tragic circumstances. His sister-in-law lay gravely ill. His mother and his two sisters must need him desperately, yet here he was standing in her small kitchen making coffee and toast for her?

'Wouldn't a message to my answering service have been simpler?'

'Would it?' he said and only had to glance at her for Shannon to know what he was getting at. He had come in person because he knew her. He'd expected her to fall apart just exactly as she had done.

Turning with the coffee pot, he went to place it on the counter next to the plate of toast, then glanced at his watch with its thick gold strap that nestled into a bed of dark hair on a wrist built to lift heavy weights if required to do so. Everything about him was built that way. The formation of his muscular structure showed the power in him yet in some unfathomable way he still managed to appear contradictorily lean and sleek.

His suit was dark, his shirt sky-blue, his tie a slender strip of navy blue silk. Wide shoulders tapered down a long lithe back to narrow hip-bones, the power in his legs and arms lay hidden beneath the expensive cut of his clothes. He could pick her up with one hand—she knew this because he had done it once when she'd challenged him. Then they'd tumbled onto the bed in a fit of laughter because one recently bathed, slippery wet and wriggling naked female was not easy to balance by her seat.

There wasn't a woman alive who didn't have heart flutters when Luca was near them. She had done more than flutter; she'd positively vibrated. He'd personified Man in her estimation and no man since him had come close to equalling him.

'Come and eat your toast.'

The dark tones in his voice made her flesh quiver. Glancing at the plate of toast, she felt a sudden desire to tell him where to go with his demonstration of concern. She didn't need him standing about her kitchen pretending that there was nothing between them but a very loose sister-brother-in-law relationship. They'd *sank* into each other's bodies for goodness' sake! He was passionately Italian and she was passionately Irish. Both stubborn, hot tempered and as temperamental as hell. Standing here watching him stroll about her kitchen was enough to ignite her temper. But common sense was telling her to just shut up and put up if she didn't want full-scale war to break out, because she knew Luca. When his mind was made up about something nothing could budge it. She had learned that the hard way.

Bitterness welled, once more she crushed it down and wondered yet again where she'd got the stupid idea from that she was over him when here she was flailing in the middle of a stomach-curdling crisis and all she seemed able to do was think about him.

Or maybe that was it, she then consoled herself as she used a trembling hand to pull out one of the two high stools that sat in front of her white laminate breakfast bar and hitched herself up onto it. Maybe obsessing about Luca was her mind's way of distracting her from what was really threatening to tear her apart.

'How are your mother and your sisters coping?' she asked as she pulled the plate of toast towards her.

'They're not,' he replied with a blunt economy that turned her stomach inside out. Then he relented slightly, sighed and added, 'They are keeping themselves occupied at the hospital, taking turns to sit with Keira and the baby. It—helps them to be there.'

'Yes.' Shannon acknowledged her acceptance of that.

Luca used that moment to pull out the other stool and sit down beside her. His thigh accidentally brushed against hers as he reached over to pour coffee into her mug. Shannon's mind went blank—although blank was nowhere near the right word to describe the sudden burning sensation that sprang to life low in her abdomen. Nor did the word suit the sudden fire-burst of images that went chasing through her head. Images of what that thigh felt like naked when brushing against her naked thigh, images of her hand stroking along its muscle-packed length and of his hand making the same sensual journey along the silken length of hers.

The old vibrations started up, running riot round her system and warming the sensitive place at her core. In an effort to pretend it just wasn't happening, she reached for a slice of toast and lifted it to her mouth. She bit but didn't taste, tried chewing though she knew she would struggle to swallow. Her mouth was too dry and she needed that coffee.

She needed him to move away so she didn't have to feel like this. She needed to remember why he was here! Oh, God, she thought wretchedly. She was ashamed of herself—she could smell him, feel him, she could even taste him! What was it with her that she couldn't keep her stupid, rotten *appalling* thoughts under control?

Her throat closed as she tried to swallow—hot, bright tears burned in her eyes. She despised herself; she despised him for coming here and doing this to her—for showing her up for the weak-willed, shallow person she had to be to be letting him get to her at a time like this when—

'Milk?' he asked.

Shannon looked at the two mugs of steaming black coffee and recalled how little it had always taken for them to want to fall upon each other. A look, a word, an accidental touch like the light brushing of thighs and they could lose themselves quite appallingly in the pleasures of the flesh. Making love with Luca had been passionate and daring and uninhibited. He had shown her pleasure she'd never known existed, lowered her so deep into her own senses that sometimes she'd struggled to float back out again.

Only twice had he actually hurt her: the first time they'd made love and the last time they'd made love. The first time Luca hadn't understood what kind of woman he'd been dealing with and she hadn't bothered to tell him that he would be her first lover so she'd accepted all the blame. When she'd cried a little afterwards he'd wrapped her in his arms and shown her a different kind of loving with the power of comfort and a need to put right what he saw as his own failure. He had done so, of course, many times and in many, many ways.

'No,' she managed to offer in answer to his question—while her mind rocketed off to recall the second time he had hurt her.

He had been blinded by fury, lost inside a frighteningly jealous rage. He had called her everything from slut to harlot and she had been so appalled that he could see her that way that she'd riled him on with biting sarcasm until he had snapped.

And it had not been the compulsive roar of sex that followed that hurt her, but the contempt with which he'd cast her aside afterwards that had ground her emotions to dust. Since then—nothing. No word, no contact—not even an acknowledgement to say that he had received back his ring.

Therefore—yes, she reiterated very grimly, she was over Luca Salvatore. The simple act of remembering those dark times was enough to kill anything she'd ever felt for him. Even if the truth came up and hit him in the face right now as they sat here pretending to be civilised and he got down on his knees to beg her forgiveness, she would not forgive.

So let her senses respond to his closeness, she invited. Let her foolish pulse quicken and her weak flesh vibrate and her shameful head try recalling the good times if it felt it had to do. But the bad times would always overshadow those good times.

'I'm going to pack a bag.' Getting up with an abruptness that startled him, she walked away without sparing his over-still, over-watchful frame a single fleeting glance.

CHAPTER TWO

LEFT alone in the kitchen, Luca stared into his mug of coffee and wondered grimly if she had actually seen him at all through that glaze of shock that covered her eyes.

Did he really care? he then questioned in outright rejection of what was rumbling around inside him. He already knew the inner Shannon too well to want to make contact again.

Been there, done that, he thought with a cold lack of any humour, then hunched forward and folded his hands around his coffee mug wishing to hell he hadn't come here. In the way he'd always believed that these things worked, life should have drawn a story on her beautiful face by now. She should look distinctly jaded but instead she was more stunningly beautiful than ever.

Lies, all lies, he contended tightly. Those too-blue eyes had turned lying into a fine art. The same with her lush, soft, kissable mouth and the way she held her chin so high whenever she allowed herself to look at him.

Challenge and contempt. He'd seen both in her face before he'd felled her with the news. What did she think gave her the right to look at him like that when she had been the one who had taken another lover into his bed?

His bed. *'Dio.'*

Letting go of his cup, he sprang to his feet on an explosion of anger and disgust, versus a strange, unwanted, stomach-clutching fight with regret.

She had been his woman. In every way he had ever looked at it he had been her man—her love, her for ever after. It had been in her eyes, in her smile, in the way she'd taken him inside her, so why—*why* had she thrown it all away?

A harsh sigh sent him to stand by the kitchen window. The rain was still lashing down outside, the night so stormy it promised to be a rough flight out of England.

Irritation shot down his backbone. Why had he come here?

He wished he knew. He wished he knew what it was that was driving him. Had he really believed that he was man enough to bury the past in this time of tragedy and deal with this situation with understanding and compassion? Or had his motives been driven by something much more basic than that—like a need to assuage this thick bloody grief churning around inside him by witnessing some sign of remorse or regret for what she had thrown away?

Well, so much for the compassion scenario because one look at her standing there at her door, one glance at the way she cowered back against the wall, and his stupid head took him back to the last time he'd seen her cower like that. So he'd pulled the lousy trick with the doors and deserved the contempt she'd thrown back at him for doing it.

And as for signs of remorse?

'*Dio,*' he grated.

He was a fool for coming here in person. He was a fool for expecting to see remorse from a woman who had shown none when she'd been caught cheating on him. He should have stayed where he belonged in Florence with his mother and sisters. He should have left a message on her cell-phone as she'd suggested— There's been a car accident, your sister is dying and my brother is dead.

'Hell,' he cursed. '*Hell!*' as his own brutal words ground his body into a clutch of agony.

Angelo—dead.

His heart began to pound like the rain on the window.

He caught sight of his own iron hard reflection washed by tears he knew he could not shed.

He turned his back on it, grabbing at his neck with tense fingers as the violence within him built like a great balloon making him want to hit something—anything to offset this black pain!

Keira and the baby—he reminded himself forcefully. Think only about them because with them there was still life and where there was life there had to be hope.

On that stern lecture he tugged his cell-phone out of his jacket pocket and stabbed in a set of numbers. Discovering the storm was ruining his signal did not improve his mood. Pocketing the phone, he went back to the sitting room to use Shannon's land-line, hoping that they wouldn't get grounded here until the storm blew over. The sooner they got to Florence, the sooner he could walk away from her.

He was amazed at how badly he needed to do that.

He heard Shannon moving about in the hall while he was still on the telephone. He kept his back to the door as he listened to what his mother was saying and kept his own voice dipped to low-toned Italian as he asked questions, received answers, and felt Shannon's stillness in the doorway like an electric charge to his spine.

The call ended, he turned. She had managed to snatch a quick shower and a change of clothes, he noticed. Gone was the sexy skirt she had been wearing, replaced by faded denims and a sweater that almost blended with her creamy skin. Her hair was up, caught in a neat knot that dowsed most of the flames. But what the prim style took away it then gave back by enhancing the delicate shape of her small oval face, her incredible blue eyes and soft little mouth, which could look Madonna-like but were really weapons of sin.

'No change,' was all he said in answer to the question he could see hovering on her lips.

No change, Shannon repeated to herself. Was that good

or bad? No change said that Keira was still hanging in there. But no change also meant that she was still in a coma, which was no reassurance at all. She wanted to know more—needed to know more and even opened her mouth to demand Luca tell her more. Then changed her mind when she was forced to accept that knowing would probably make her fall apart again and she had to keep herself together if she wanted to get through the long hours of travelling that lay ahead.

So she made her voice sound composed when she said, 'I need to use the phone if you've finished with it. I have to let some people know that I won't be around for a while.'

A nod of his dark head and Luca took a step sideways. Dark clothes, dark eyes, dark everything, he seemed to cast a heavy shadow across her light and airy room. Picking up the receiver, she felt the heat from his grasp still lingering. For some stupid reason, feeling the intimacy that heat evoked made her throat ache all the more as she tapped in the number of her co-partner at the busy graphic design company she and Joshua Soames had built together.

As she murmured huskily, 'Hi, Josh, it's me…' Luca turned and walked out of the room. His shadow remained, though, casting a pall over everything. Taking a deep breath in preparation for a shower of sympathy and concern she just didn't want to have to deal with right now, she began to explain.

Luca reappeared while she was making her second call to confirm that her neighbour still had the spare key to her flat so she could keep an eye on it for her.

'Thanks, Alex, I owe you one,' she murmured gratefully. 'Dinner when I get back? Sure, my shout. It will be something to look forward to.'

The dull throb of silence returned once she'd replaced the receiver. Luca was shrugging into his overcoat and his profile could have been cast in iron. 'Anyone else?' he asked

and, at her reply, he flashed her a hard smile. 'Only the tw
men in your life? You are a consistent little thing, Shannon
I will say that.'

Her response was to walk away without giving him th
satisfaction of answer. His reasons to be bitter—imagine
or otherwise—were his prerogative, but his right to tak
cheap shots at her now, when other things were so muc
more important, filled her with fresh contempt. She wasn'
going to explain that Alex was a woman and that Josh wa
the man who'd saved her life when *Luca* had done his bes
to ruin it!

He was standing by the front door when she came out o
her bedroom wearing a long black woollen coat and a ha
pulled down over her ears, both of which had become es
sential accessories during the winter the UK was endurin
this year.

'Is this it?' he asked without making eye contact. In on
hand he held her suitcase, in the other the padded black ba
that contained her laptop computer.

Settling the strap to her handbag on her shoulder, 'Yes,
she replied. 'Do you have a car outside or do we need t
use mine?'

'I have a hire car.'

Turning away, he opened the door and stepped out ont
the landing, then went to call the lift while Shannon locke
up her flat. They rode the lift like perfect strangers, and le
the building to walk into driving rain. Luckily his hire ca
waited only a few yards away. Using a remote control t
unlock it, he swung open the passenger door to allo
Shannon to get in and out of the rain before he strode roun
to the boot to stash her things, finally arriving behind th
wheel wet through.

Neither had thought to catch up one of the umbrellas sh
kept by the front door. Neither seemed to give a damn. A
the car engine fired Shannon turned her face to the sid

window. With only a swipe from a hand across his wet face, Luca ignored the raindrops running down the back of his neck and set them moving with the grim desire to get this over with as quickly as it was humanly possible.

He was angry with himself for making that comment about her personal life. It had placed him in the position of sounding hard and nasty, and could have given the impression that he cared when he didn't. She could have as many Alexes as she liked lining up to take their turn in her bed. Joshua Soames was a different matter. Luca knew all about her close friend and business partner because Keira never ceased to talk about how their graphic design venture had taken off like a rocket from the moment the two of them had begun to trade. The two partners had been friends throughout university, both excelling in computer design. Luca had listened to Keira spouting proud things about her sister even that far back. Only his mood had been more indulgent then—his mind remembering a rather cute, if self-conscious, freckle-faced teenager with a head of gorgeous hair in a pale blue taffeta bridesmaid's dress that managed to wear her rather than the other way around. She'd simply amused him then. He'd *liked* her because despite all her teenage awkwardness she'd had a tongue like a whip, which had entertained him all the way through Keira and Angelo's long wedding breakfast.

Needless to say it was the image he'd used to conjure up of Shannon whenever Keira had mentioned her younger sister. So when, four years later, she'd arrived on her first visit to Florence and he'd found himself confronted by the grown-up version, he had been completely blown away.

Beautiful, he thought, and tightened his grip on the steering wheel. Astoundingly, fascinatingly beautiful. The freckles had gone; her body had filled out to take on a shape that was truly spectacular. And instead of teenage awkwardness he'd been faced with a supremely self-confident graduate with a hunger for life and lethal gift for flirtation. She'd plied him with coquettish looks and her plans to start up her own design company with Joshua Soames and take the world by storm. Older, wiser, and as cynical as hell abou people with ideals so grand, he'd listened patiently, an swered all her eager questions about financial management and found it was *he* who was taken by storm.

The first time they'd kissed it had been meant as a broth erly salutation to finish off the evening they'd just spen together listening to Puccini. She had been eager to go to the opera and he had been happy to take her. They'd shared a candlelit dinner at his favourite restaurant afterwards and even though he had known by then that he was getting in too deep, he had held onto the arrogant belief that he stil had control of the situation—until that kiss.

Grimly driving them out of the city now in weather so foul a duck would find shelter, he felt his lips heat at the memory. He had not intended it to be a meaningful kiss just one of those light exchanges you shared with someone you'd spent a pleasant evening with. But Shannon had faller into that kiss with the same all-out enthusiasm she threw a life. It had shaken him, sent his libido soaring to a place i had never known was there.

Bringing the car to a halt at a junction, he checked the road either way and used the opportunity to cast a brie glance at her. She was sitting there with her head turned away and that silly little hat pulled down over her ears Something hot shot from his heart to his loins, then stayed burning there. Only Shannon had ever made that connection only she had ever been able to turn him into a mass o raging hormones without needing to try.

Ten years his junior, yet divided by almost a millen nium's difference in life experience, she'd caught him trussed him up and packaged him in a box marked 'taken'— by the woman with the amazing hair, the stunning face, fantastic body and an insatiable set of desires that had him balancing on the edge of fear that she might decide to find satisfaction elsewhere.

Well, he'd got his wish, if that was what he had been looking for. And he should have been relieved he'd found out before he'd placed the wedding ring on her finger. Yet oddly he hadn't been—not once the first flush of anger had worn off, that was. All he'd felt then was regret because at least a wedding ring would have given him a reason to go after her—haul her back by her lovely hair and make her pay for daring to betray him.

Instead he'd enjoyed two years of long, hard, festering about what should have been. And in that time bitterness had turned his view of women so sour he hadn't been able to touch one since.

A great legacy for her to chew on, if she ever found out she'd rendered him impotent, he grimaced as they drove through rain like sheets of ice.

If he throws me one more nasty look I think I might turn round and hit him, Shannon decided as she sat watching his profile via the side-window reflection. Up to now she had watched him slice her one look of utter blinding derision, several of disgust and two of seething sexual denunciation. The roads were bad enough without him distracting himself from his driving by thinking lewd and hateful thoughts.

A slave to his ever-raging libido, she thought. Sex was all that Luca knew. Not *Love* but *Sex*—give me, I need, I want, I have to have. Physical, insatiable, inventive and so good at it that it was no wonder his reputation went before him. Variety—he used to say while grinning unrepentantly when she used to face him with grapevine chatter—is most definitely the spice of life. She should have realised then that she was nothing but a brand new and exciting variety he simply had to try out.

Love? Not this man. He had no idea of the concept if it

didn't attach itself to some physical act. The word? Oh, he'd known how to use the necessary words to gain the required responses. I love you. *Ti amo mio per sempre l'innamorato.* Whispered words in sensual Italian that could seduce a woman to mush.

Then suddenly she was a slut and a harlot, a woman beneath his dignity to know. One mistake—not even *her* mistake—and she had been put out in the cold so fast, she was still dealing with the shock of it two years later.

Over him? she asked. No, she wasn't over him. She was still too angry, bitter and hungry to draw blood to be anywhere near getting *over* what Luca had done to her.

'We will never take off in this weather,' he gritted.

Tears pricked her eyes at the sudden realisation that she had allowed herself to concentrate on Luca instead of on Keira yet again. Oh, may God forgive me, she thought and had to rummage in her bag for a tissue.

'You OK?' Luca had heard her telling little snuffle.

'Fine,' she said, hating him—hating him with every fiber she was made of.

'Not far to the airport,' he said more levelly.

He knew she was crying. But then, he knew her so well. Inside, outside, every which way a man could know a woman he had lived and slept with for half a year before he'd chucked her out. Gritting his teeth together, Luca withdrew inside himself, dark eyes fierce as they pierced the driving rain in his quest to get to the airport and out of close contact with the hate of his life. He had never been more relieved as he was when he saw the lights of the private airport where his plane was waiting for them. He needed some space—air to breathe that wasn't tainted with the scent of this woman.

The hire-car parking bay was under cover. Getting out, he directed Shannon to the departure lounge, then headed off in the other direction to officially hand back the car keys.

By the time he went looking for her, she had removed her hat and coat and was standing in front of the departure lounge viewing window watching the rain pelting down from the sky.

Five feet eight was fairly tall for a woman, but next to him Shannon felt small, frail, delicate. Tonight as he paused to study her slender legs encased in denim and the pale sweater she was wearing he could detect a new fragility in the slender lines of her figure. It was a frailty caused by vulnerability and fear, and realising it made him feel the worst kind of lout for letting his feelings towards her get the better of him.

Smothering the urge to heave out a self-aimed angry sigh, he decided to make it easy on both of them and give her a wide berth. Walking over to the bar, he ordered a stiff drink then remained leaning there staring down at it without drinking, unaware that Shannon had watched his reflection in the window, every grim step of the way.

He hates being here with me as much as I hate him being here, she was thinking heavily, and wished she understood why knowing that caused such a terrible ache deep down inside. She didn't love him—didn't even want to be near him any more, so she was glad when he remained by the bar instead of coming near her—wasn't she?

Forcing her eyes to focus further out into the night, she concentrated on watching the rain hitting the airport lights with almost enough power to smash the glass, while the wind buffeted madly at everything. And inside she prayed fervently that the weather would clear so they could be on their way to what really mattered.

Keira, her beloved Keira, the new baby—and poor, poor Angelo.

Maybe the fates decided to take pity on them because half an hour later Luca appeared at her shoulder. 'They think there is a hole coming in the storm,' he informed her. 'If we can board and be ready, then we might be given the chance to get away from here.'

Getting away sounded so good to her that Shannon instantly turned and went to collect her belongings from the nearby chair where she had placed them. Shrugging into her coat, she pulled on her hat while Luca pulled on his coat. Five minutes later and they were walking side by side yet a million miles apart in every other way.

Magically, halfway to the Salvatore jet the rain suddenly stopped, the wind died away and glancing up Shannon saw the stars appear through a hole in the scurrying clouds. The break in the weather helped to lift some of her fears about Keira. She was going to be all right, Shannon promised herself firmly—*willing* it to be so.

'Choose a seat and belt yourself in,' Luca instructed as soon as they entered the plane. 'I am going to check with my pilot.'

Even as he finished speaking he was disappearing through a door at the other end of the cabin and a flight attendant appeared to take her outdoor things. The man must have known that this was no pleasure trip because his expression remained sober, and once he had quietly suggested the best place for her to sit in the plush cream leather interior he disappeared, leaving her to make herself comfortable in peace.

Two minutes later the plane left the ground and shot towards the star-scattered hole in the clouds. An hour after that and Luca hadn't put in an appearance. Deciding he was deliberately keeping out of her way the same as he had done in the airport departure lounge, Shannon finally felt able to relax the guard she'd been keeping on herself, and almost immediately felt her eyelids begin to droop.

Maybe it was for the best if she slept through some of the journey, she consoled herself after trying to fight the urge for a little while. It might feel as if she was abandoning some kind of vigil she had been maintaining for her sister, but common sense told her that stuck up here she couldn't be more helpless if she tried to be.

So she let herself go, dreamed of her Keira's familiar light laughter and of sweet-smelling babies. She held her vigil there in her dreams, where everyone was whole and healthy and no dark forces came to disturb the beauty of it.

Luca sat watching her for a while, feeling oddly disturbed by how peaceful she was. She used to sleep like this, he recalled. Lying so quiet and still beside him that he'd sometimes had to fight the urge to lean over her and check that she was still breathing. A foolish notion when he had been holding her in his arms and could feel her living warmth pulsing softly against him.

Dio, stop thinking about it, he told himself and pushed his head back into the seat cushion, then closed his eyes and tried to relax. But ugly scenes began playing on the backs of his eyelids, forcing him to open them again.

Angelo—Angelo… He shifted restlessly. Men didn't weep. He wanted to weep. He wanted his brother back so he could let him know one last time how much he meant to him.

Tears began to burn like acid. He got up, hurried down the length of the cabin, then turned to pace restlessly back again. This had been the worst day of his life and it still was not over. He felt as if he had spent the day travelling the world carrying bad news like the grim reaper. He'd broken the news to his mother, to his sisters Renata and Sophia, then taken their disapproval with him to fly to London to break the news to Shannon. Now here he was flying home again with his passenger, who clearly found escape in sleep a better option than staying awake to talk to him.

Did he want to talk to Shannon about anything? he asked himself suddenly.

No, he did not.

Did he want her to wake up?

No, to that question too.

He paced away again, then turned and grimly made his way back to her side. She still hadn't moved a single eyelash. Her face was relaxed but very pale. Her lips were together, soft and flushed with their usual rose-like bloom, but if she was breathing through her nose then he could see no evidence of it, no hint that her breasts were moving up and down.

Don't be a fool, man! he told himself harshly. You know how she sleeps—you *know*! Yet still he found himself leaning over her to place light fingertips against her pale cheek.

Shannon came out of her haven of sleep to find Luca standing over her. He was so close she could feel his breath on her face. Their eyes clashed, two years shot away with the force of a gun crack and she was looking into his face as it had once looked minutes after his loving, one that had shattered her for ever. She saw anger, the contempt and dismay. She saw eyes turned black with the same emotion that had been driving him and felt the full wretched impact of hurt surge up once again.

Tears flooded into her eyes. 'I hate you,' she choked and struck out at him on impulse with a trembling clenched fist.

'Hate?' he echoed and caught the fist before it could land, closing it inside an iron grip. 'You do not understand the meaning of the word,' he bit back harshly. 'This, *cara*, is hate—'

With a tug he yanked her up against him, aiming her mouth up to his so that they collided, and he smothered her shrill cry of protest with the demanding thrust of his tongue. He kissed her in anger, he kissed her in punishment, but it was the heat of his passion that set her struggling wildly to break free. An arm snaked around her waist and she found herself standing with the front of her body clamped to his.

Her fist was released so that he could claim the back of her head and maintain the pressure of the kiss.

He ravished her mouth; he uttered thick curses deep in his throat. Her hair came loose to tumble around his fingers. He kissed her and kissed her until she stopped fighting and started trembling. Two years of abstinence and the reasons for it didn't matter any more because they were back where they'd left off, at war with each other and using sex as their weapon. She scraped her nails down his shirt front, she scored them into his hair, their lips moved in a hungry, sensuous feasting—then as suddenly as it had begun it finished.

Luca thrust her away so violently that she landed in a huddle back in her seat. Dizzy and disorientated, shocked beyond trying to think, Shannon watched him spin on his heel and stride down the cabin. When he reached the far end he picked up what looked like a bottle of whisky, poured some liquid into a glass, then tossed it to the back of his throat.

Staring at the rigid set of his shoulders, she wanted to say something—spit insults at him for daring to grab and kiss her just to prove a stupid point. But her lips felt hot and bruised and she was shaking so badly inside that she didn't think she could make the words coherent. Instead she lowered her face into her hands, let her hair fall around her like a curtain and prayed that he had been too busy punishing her to notice that she had been kissing him back.

The silence after that was like a razor blade slicing through every second they had left to travel. They landed under clear, dark Italian skies but it was cold enough for Shannon to be glad of her warm coat.

Luca had left his car in the airport car park. Shannon climbed into the passenger seat leaving Luca to stow her things. They drove towards Florence in total silence; their only exchange of words since the kiss in the cabin had been his terse information that he'd rung the hospital and there was still no change.

Familiar landmarks began to flash by her window. They were nearing Florence and the closer they got to the city, the more anxious Shannon became. Eventually the car slowed and turned in through an entrance in a high stuccoed wall. Shannon saw a building which, despite the gardens neatly surrounding it, still had the look that all hospitals had, even if this one was obviously a very exclusive place to be ill.

As Luca brought the car to a halt her skin began to prickle. Taking a deep breath in an effort to brace herself she unlocked her seat belt and got out. Her legs began to shake as she walked towards the hospital entrance. Luca came to walk alongside her but made no attempt to touch.

She didn't want him to touch her, she told herself. But the moment she stepped into the hushed hospital foyer she was having second thoughts about that. Luca indicated towards the lifts. As they stepped into one Shannon began to feel strange—alien to herself almost.

Maybe he sensed it because as the lift doors closed them both inside, he questioned, 'OK?'

She nodded, swallowing on the build-up of tension that had begun to collect in her throat. Her body was tense, her flesh creeping with feelings no one, unless they were about to face a similar situation, could begin to understand. And she was pale; she knew she was pale because her face felt so cold and washed out.

'Don't be alarmed by the amount of equipment you will find surrounding her,' Luca seemed compelled to warn. 'It is standard practice in cases like these to monitor just about everything they can…'

He was trying to prepare her. It was all she could do to give a jerky nod of her head in response. The lift stopped

Her heart began to pump so oddly that it made it difficult to draw breath.

The doors slid open on a foyer similar to the one they'd walked through downstairs—and Shannon's courage seemed to drop like a stone to her feet, stopping her from moving another inch.

She closed her eyes, tried to swallow again, felt her breasts lifting and falling on small tight gasps for air as a stark sense of dread closed her in. Then the lift pinged, giving notice that it was about to close its doors again. Her eyes flickered upwards at the same time that Luca shot out an arm—not towards her but to hold back those impatient doors.

His eyes were fixed on her, narrowed slightly and shadowed by concern. His face was pale, lips slightly parted on tense white teeth as if he was struggling to control an urge to make a grab for her.

'I'm all right,' she breathed in whispered assurance. 'Just give me a second to—'

'Take your time,' he said gruffly. 'There is no rush.'

No? Shannon fretfully contradicted that assertion. She might already be too late!

Too late... She groaned in silent agony. Too late belonged to the years she had avoided coming anywhere near Florence. Too late belonged to the way she had cut Keira right out of her life for months and even after they'd made up—in a fashion—she'd kept her strictly at an arm's length by being cool, being remote, piling on the guilt and the—

The lift gave another ping and kept on pinging, trying to close its doors against Luca's blocking arm. On a mammoth dragging-together of her courage Shannon made herself move. The first person she saw was Luca's mother. She looked dreadful, her beautifully defined face withered by anxiety and grief.

The ever-ready tears rushed into Shannon's eyes again,

her voice wobbling on the words that had to be said. 'I'm so sorry about Angelo, Mrs Salvatore,' she murmured in unsteady Italian as she moved on instinct, reaching out with her arms to draw the poor woman in an embrace.

It took a few seconds to realise that the embrace was not welcome. Stiff and unbending, Mrs Salvatore was accepting of her touch out of politeness—but that was all. As Shannon drew away, shaken by the cold reminder of how Luca's family felt about her, she saw the other faces bearing witness to her rejection.

Then Luca stepped up behind her, bringing his hands up to curve her shoulders in what Shannon could only describe as a declaration of some kind. He didn't say a single word, but all eyes lifted to his face, then dropped away uncomfortably.

'To your left,' he quietly instructed her.

Dry-mouthed, inwardly struck to her core, Shannon forced herself to start walking again. With Luca's hand still curving her slender nape and with a new kind of silence thickening the air, they entered a corridor that put the rest of his family out of view—thankfully, because she didn't need any cold witnesses when she faced what was to come.

And it came quickly—too quickly. Through the very first door they encountered, in fact. Luca paused, so did she, watching as he pushed the door open then gently urged her to move again. Her body felt heavy, that sense of dark dread placing a drag on her limbs as she made herself step through the opening into a well-lit room with white walls and staffed by a white-uniformed nurse who stood by a white-sheeted bed.

And then there was the white-faced creature lying in the bed.

CHAPTER THREE

IT WAS the point when her control split wide open. Shannon had thought she was prepared, she'd truly believed she was ready to deal with whatever she had to face in this room. But she found she couldn't cope with the sight of her sister lying there so pale and still as if life's essence itself was slowly seeping out of her.

The choked sob that attempted to escape had to be rammed back into her mouth by a shaking fist at the same moment that she took a staggering step backwards, pressing herself against the full muscle-packed length of Luca, who acted like a wall to halt her cowardly retreat. Eyes blurred, throat thick, mouth trembling, she fought to get a hold on herself.

It was awful. It took a fierce effort to force herself forward on legs that didn't feel supportive. Arriving at the side of the bed, she reached for one of her sister's limp hands. It felt warm and that was comforting. Warmth meant life.

'Keira?' she called out unsteadily. 'Keira—it's Shannon. Can she hear me?' she demanded of the nurse. Then, before the woman could answer, her attention honed right back on the white face lying against white pillows. 'Oh, Keira,' she burst out painfully. 'Wake up and talk to me!'

'Here…' a deep voice prompted. A pair of hands carefully eased the overcoat from her shoulders, then a chair arrived at the back of her knees, giving her no choice but to sit.

The diversion stopped her from falling apart as, she realised, she had been about to do. 'H-how deeply unconscious is she?' she asked huskily.

'Some of it is drug induced,' Luca offered with what she supposed was meant to be a comfort. The nurse seemed to have slipped away, making her exit without Shannon noticing.

'Has she woken up at all since the accident?'

'No,' Luca answered gruffly.

'Does that mean she doesn't even know she's had her baby?'

'No,' he said again.

Shannon felt her insides begin to burn as a whole new set of emotions went raging through her blood. How many failed pregnancies had poor Keira endured through the years before she'd managed to carry this baby to almost full term? Five or six, Shannon was sure, since she'd married Angelo.

Would a girl child be enough for her? With her own life hanging in the balance here, would her sister now give up on her obsession to give Angelo a male heir?

Angelo—what was she thinking? There was no more Angelo. 'Oh, Keira,' she whispered painfully. How was she going to cope without her beloved Angelo?

Then began long hours of torment. Nothing around her felt real. She sat by the bed and talked to Keira. When she was gently removed from the room by medical staff who needed to check Keira, she sat outside in the corridor and lost herself in grief for Angelo. Occasionally Luca would appear, or his mother or one of the sisters. It didn't occur to her that she was never left entirely on her own or that the family attitude towards her had taken a complete about turn. Perhaps, if she had noticed, she would have started to realise that their sharing of her vigil was a bad sign. But she didn't notice and she rarely spoke, unless it was to Keira—then she talked and talked and talked without remembering a single word.

At one point someone gently asked her if she would like to see the baby. She thought she should do, for Keira's sake, but that was all. So she agreed and was utterly blown away by the tiny scrap of human life lying in her clear plastic cocoon fighting her own little battle.

Keira's daughter—Angelo and Keira's.

She burst into a flood of tears and wept for everyone, her emotions like a driverless vehicle wildly out of control. When she went back to sit with Keira her voice was as calm as a slow-running stream as she talked and talked and talked.

'You've had enough—'

The light touch on her shoulder brought Shannon's limp head lifting from the crisp white sheet that she had not been aware of resting against. Sleep-starved eyes blinked uncomprehendingly up into a determined gaze that was brown flecked with gold.

'You can do no more here tonight, Shannon,' Luca said quietly. 'It is time for us to leave and get some rest now.'

'I...' can be here, she was about to insist, but Luca silenced her with a shake of his head.

'Keira is stable,' he stated firmly. 'The people here know where to contact us if they need to. It is time for us to leave.'

The voice of authority, she recognised. Luca was not going to take no for an answer and if she was honest she knew he was right. She was so utterly used up she was barely functioning on any sensible level.

But it felt like desertion when she made herself get up from the chair and she lifted up one of Keira's hands and pressed a soft kiss to it before leaning over to leave another kiss on her cheek.

'Love you,' she whispered, then she was turning to walk away with wretched tears blurring her progress to the door with Luca following close behind.

'Where are you going?'

She blinked, her sleep-starved brain taking whole seconds to realise they were now outside her sister's room, the door having been pulled shut so silently she hadn't even heard it. 'The baby,' she murmured, waving a decidedly uncoordinated hand in the direction of the nursery. 'I want to...'

'The baby is fine,' he assured. 'I have been with her for the last hour while you sat with Keira.'

An hour? Shannon blinked again. Luca had been with the baby for a whole hour? The picture that produced in her head just didn't correspond somehow with the man she thought she knew.

'I watched the nurse attend to her, then they let me hold her for a while...'

Something passed over his face, a wave of unchecked emotion that emphasised the ring of pain that was circling at his mouth. Guilt made a sudden clutching grab at her aching heart. This man had just lost his beloved brother but, while she had been selfishly absorbed in her sister's plight, Luca had been too busy supporting others to find the time to deal with his own loss. She had been existing in a fog since they'd arrived here, but he'd split his time between comforting his grief-stricken mother or one of his two sisters as well as attending to her.

Now here he stood, doing what he did best: being the strong Salvatore male. But when she looked into his eyes she saw the desolation beneath his glossy black lashes. She also witnessed another painful image of him slipping away to go to the nursery to hold a tiny baby girl who was the only link to his brother.

Her heart ached again, everything ached, for Luca as well as herself.

'Oh, Luca,' she murmured as impulse made her take a step closer to him with soft words of sympathy trembling up from her throat.

He saw it coming. His face closed up. 'Here,' he clipped. 'Put this on...'

He held out her coat. Shannon stared at it, aware that

she'd just had a door slammed shut in her face again. And why not? she asked herself bleakly as she swallowed the words of comfort and felt the tremor that came with them shiver its way to her feet. Her sister was alive but his brother was dead. Accepting comfort from his ex-lover-turned-enemy would be a blow to his dignity he could do without.

So she let him feed her coat sleeves up her arms without uttering another syllable. As the heavy garment settled on her tired shoulders she pushed her hands into its deep pockets to hug the warm wool around her, then walked towards the bank of lifts. The chairs in the foyer were empty now; the rest of the Salvatore family had been sent home to their beds long ago.

The silence between them held as they drove away into the cool dark night. A glance at the clock illuminated on the car dashboard told it was one o'clock in the morning. It felt as if a whole week had gone by since she'd got out of bed yesterday at six in the morning and rushed out to catch the commuter flight to Paris. Such a lot had happened since then. Too much—too much, she thought dully as she rested her head against the soft leather headrest, then closed her hot, tired, gritty eyes.

Luca watched as she slipped into an exhausted slumber and grimaced to himself. He knew the impression he had given her back there in the hospital, but she could not be more wrong about his motives if she'd tried. However, receiving comfort from a warm and sympathetic Shannon right now would have shattered the control he was hanging onto by a thread.

And it was not over yet—though he was aware that Shannon didn't know that. There was more to come—a battle—he predicted, because she was not going to like it when she discovered where she was staying. Let his defences drop before the fight was won and he would turn himself into a target for someone of Shannon's fiercely stubborn independent nature.

Dio, he thought tiredly as he drove them through the silent streets of Florence. He was not that sure that he wasn't already that target. A mere glance at her sitting beside him with her long legs stretched out in front of her, the white oval of her face so exquisite in repose, he experienced that telling needle-sharp sting of Man on the prowl.

She got to him. She always had done. Love or hate her, he *always* wanted her and it was knowing that that made him such a target. Give her reason to spark and he was going to catch a light. He was so sure of it that he would try anything to keep her asleep until he had her safely ensconced in a bed—and he'd put himself on the other side of the bedroom door.

A sitting duck. Angelo's words, he remembered starkly. Angelo had said that the two of them were both targets for a pair of Irish witches to enchant at will.

Angelo… A collapse took place inside his chest. It was a sensation he had grown familiar with during this long, miserable day. He missed his brother—already. He wanted Angelo back. Tears stung hot and dry against the backs of his eyes and he felt his skin stretch across his cheek-bones with tension.

His foot hit the accelerator, using a surge of unnecessary bodily power to release the pressure in his chest. Familiar landmarks flashed by the side window. He saw a set of traffic lights ahead glowing red; he aimed for them—felt the burning rush swell inside him, challenging that bastard called death. It was compelling, seductive.

Shannon stirred. He glanced at her, saw beauty personified in his stark eyes and, clenching his jaw tight and gritting his teeth, he forced himself to slow down. One car crash in the family was enough. The moment of madness eased, leaving Shannon still asleep beside him with no idea how close he'd come to putting her safety at risk.

The sensation remained, though, burning like acid in his gut, anger at the waste of his brother's life overlaying the numbing sense of grief. It was going to need assuaging and he had a grim suspicion he knew by what source.

It was feeling the car swing sharply down a steep incline that stirred Shannon awake. Opening red-rimmed eyes, she sat up to peer out at the lines of cars parked in the basement car park and, as Luca slotted the car into its reserved parking slot, he waited for recognition to spark.

It didn't happen. Probably too tired to notice anything much, she yawned then opened her door and stepped out. He did the same, eyeing her carefully as she waited in weary silence for him to recover her luggage then walked beside him to the lift.

They stepped into it together. While he used a plastic security card to activate the lift she went to lean against one of the metal cased walls, thrust her hands into her coat pockets, then proceeded to stare at her booted feet.

'You have access, then,' she remarked, smothering yet another yawn.

'Yes, I have access,' was all he said.

'Good of them.'

'Hmm?'

'Angelo and Keira. It's good of them to trust you with security access to their apartment.'

He didn't answer, keeping his expression blank while he wondered if she was even aware that she'd used his brother's name as if Angelo were still alive.

That anger stirred again; he crushed it down. The lift began to rise. He wanted to hit something and wished he didn't feel like this.

'But then, that's nothing new,' she added with a sudden

tinge of bitterness in her voice. 'Security access to each others' homes has always been the norm for the Salvatores.'

'You think that's a bad thing?'

'I think it's bloody stupid,' she replied. 'I know Italian families like to be close, but having the right to walk in and out of each others' homes when they feel like it is taking family unity to the extreme.'

'Because you were once caught out by this—extreme perhaps?'

The taunt hit home. She flinched, then lifted her chin to send him a clear cold stare. He countered it with a thin smile. Mutual antipathy began to sing. The lift stopped. She was so busy defying him to take that comment further that when the lift doors slid open she still did not notice where she was.

So he said nothing and merely mocked her with a gesture of his hand to step out of the lift. Head up, eyes like ice, she walked forward, stooping to collect up her bags from where they sat at his feet before saying tightly. 'Goodnight, Luca. I'm sure you know your own way out again.'

Then she walked—or did she flounce? Luca mused curiously. Whichever, she did it sensationally in her ankle-length coat and flaming red hair; it was almost a shame that reality was about to spoil it.

She was several strides in before she began to take in the décor of rich cream walls and inlaid wood floors on which stood the kind of heavy antique pieces that she would never have connected with Keira's more homely tastes.

Luca watched her freeze, watched her take stock, watched her pull in a sharp breath before she spun to stare at him as he slid the plastic security card back into his leather wallet while the lift doors closed behind his blocking frame.

'No,' she breathed in stricken protest. 'I'm not staying here with you, Luca. No way.'

It took fewer strides to bring her back to him. Eyes bright

with defiance, she snaked a hand over his shoulder to gave the lift-call button a firm press.

'It won't come without my authorisation,' he reminded her gently.

'Then authorise it.'

She was standing so close that he could feel her breath on his face. She smelled of Chanel and the hospital, and the tumbled untidiness of her hair flamed like a warning around her face. She was trying her best to defy him but underneath the defiance he knew alarm bells were ringing because she did not understand his motives for bringing her here of all places, back to the scene of the crime, so to speak.

He could reassure her that he had nothing sinister on his mind and that she had to stay somewhere and even he wasn't so brutal that he take her to a dead man's house then leave her there alone—but it would not be the truth. Something had happened to him during the mad drive here, and he now wanted her so badly that it burned in his gut like a pounding fever. He wanted to pick her up and throw her over his shoulder, find the nearest bed and drop her down on it, then follow with some good, hard sex. No preliminaries, just a quick, hot slaking of all this *stuff* he was struggling to deal with: his brother, her sister—Shannon back here and within his reach. She had made the last two years of his life a misery—the least she could do in reparation was help him assuage his grief!

Shannon knew what he was thinking—it was vibrating all around them like some dark, compelling force. The desire, the old burning attraction, that needle-sharp prick of sexual awareness that made his eyes glow gold and made her need to run the tip of her tongue around the sudden dry curve of her lips.

'No,' she breathed in husky denial.

'Why not?' He watched that telling little gesture and smiled. 'For old time's sake.'

For old time's sake? Her own affronted gasp almost choked her. She couldn't believe he was behaving like this! Didn't it matter to him that there was a life-threatening situation taking place not far away, or that one person had died and another two were fighting a battle with death?

'You ought to be ashamed of yourself,' she told him, then turned on her heel and walked away across the large square entrance hall with all its familiar trappings of wealth, like the exquisite antique chest set against one wall with the magnificent bronze statue of Apollo standing on its top. She strode beneath the wide archway through which she gained access to the rest of the apartment. And she walked with purpose, knowing exactly where she was making for.

The kitchen, which led to the utility room, which in turn led to the rear exit door. A locked rear exit door, she soon discovered. Her heart sank—but not her resolve, she determined as she dropped her bags to the floor then turned, eyes wearing such a hard glint now that they should have turned him to stone where he stood propping up the other door, watching her lazily.

'I'll get out,' she warned, 'if I have to break windows.'

'We are four floors up,' he reminded her.

'Broken windows upset people,' she explained, undeterred. 'They tend to call in the police when glass comes showering down on top of them.'

His hard mouth gave a mocking twist. 'Well, that might have been fun,' he drawled. 'If the glass wasn't shatterproof.'

Her shoulders sagged; this was getting stupid. 'Look,' she snapped. 'It's late. I'm tired—you're tired. We've both had a rotten day! Can we just stop this now?' She tried a bit of pleading. 'Let me out of here, Luca—please!'

'I wish it was that simple,' he grimaced.

'It is!' she insisted.

'No, it isn't,' he returned with a snap that altered his

taunting mood to the grimly serious. 'So let's get a couple of things straight. You are staying here in my apartment, because it is situated so close to the hospital—'

'I'd rather stay at Angelo and Keira's place.'

He stiffened suddenly, dark eyes flaring up with a blistering rage. 'Angelo is dead!' he barked at her. 'So will you stop dotting his name into every damn sentence, for goodness' sake?'

Shannon blinked in surprise, her face turning as white as a sheet. Had she been doing that? She hadn't been aware of it. When she thought about her sister she automatically put Angelo with her. Angelo and Keira—it had always been that way. 'I'm s-sorry,' she stammered, not knowing what else to say.

Luca frowned. 'Forget I said that,' he dismissed, then sucked in a deep breath. 'The point is,' he went on, 'that Angelo and Keira have moved since you were last here. It is now more than an hour's drive out of the city to their new home. My mother is not fit to be on her own right now so she has gone to stay with Sophia, which leaves you with a choice, Shannon,' he offered finally. 'You either stay here with me, stay with Renata, or you go and stay with my mother at Sophia's house.'

Which was absolutely no choice at all, she acknowledged heavily. His mother hated her. So did his sisters. Staying with them would be just a different kind of hell. And anyway, his family had a right to do their grieving together and without an unwanted interloper in their midst.

'There are such things as hotels, you know,' she pointed out stubbornly.

'Are you really so selfish that you would go to a hotel knowing that such a choice would not only offend my mother, but would hurt Keira beyond all that is fair if and when she discovers it?' He sent her a look that stung. 'She will blame the family, she will blame me for not being man enough to put my own feelings about you to one side for her sake.'

'But you aren't putting your feelings aside!' she cried.

'I will if you will.'

'Liar,' she breathed. But as for the rest he was, oh, so frustratingly right that, on acceptance, her ability to remain standing upright any longer disintegrated and she sank wearily against the locked door behind her and dropped her face into her hands.

It was a surrender. He knew it and well and she knew it. But Shannon could not resist dropping one final comment into the throbbing silence that fell. 'I hate you,' she whispered from the all-enveloping shield of her tumbling hair.

'No, you don't,' Luca denied. 'You still fancy the hell out of me and that, *cara*, is what you hate.'

'That's a lie!' The hands dropped so she could spit the disclaimer at him.

'Is it?' His eyes were cold now, hardened by his arrogant belief in what he was claiming. 'Cast your mind back to the kiss on the flight over here,' he suggested. 'If I had not stopped it you would have gone up in a plume of smoke.'

'My God,' she gasped. 'You conceited devil!'

'Maybe.' He gave an indifferent shrug. 'But I know what I know.'

'You kissed me, if you remember!'

'And you fell into it as you always did,' he declared with contempt.

'And you didn't—?'

His grimace conceded that point to her. 'It is going to be really interesting for us to see if we can both survive the next few days without falling on each other again, don't you think?'

'I think you're disgusting!'

A black brow arched, he ran his eyes down the slender body he could see between the gaping sides of her coat.

'Are your breasts tight, Shannon?' he questioned softly. 'Is that place between your legs getting all hot and anxious because we are talking about it?'

She launched herself away from the door with a need to slap his taunting face!

'Sex in the utility room, now that's a new turn-on,' he drawled as she flew towards him. 'But then you never did have any inhibitions as to where or with whom you did it so long as you did.'

Each word was aimed to draw blood from its victim, each mocking glint in his dark eyes was meant to drive her over the edge. She stopped a foot away, trying to push down the rage tumbling around inside her because a part of her was aware that he was provoking her deliberately. His eyes were goading her; his whole lazy, taunting stance was just begging her to take that swipe at him.

'I don't understand why you're doing this,' she breathed unsteadily.

He laughed; it wasn't a pleasant sound. 'Maybe I'm curious as to how much you've learned since you moved on to pastures new.'

'Stop it,' she whispered.

But he wasn't going to stop anything. 'Did you tempt him as you used to tempt me, Shannon?' he questioned curiously. 'Did you tease him into showing you yet another way to reach that mind-blowing final thrill?'

Her arm came up between the glare of their eyes, fixed and warring, and she let fly with her hand. He caught it before it landed its blow, hard fingers closing around her slender wrist to keep the hand suspended a small half-inch from his face.

'We both know that the thrill was all you ever really wanted from me,' he continued remorselessly, 'but did you think you'd exhausted all *my* possibilities? Wrong, darling.' He dared to kiss the tips of her clawing fingers. 'We never so much as scratched the surface. You have no idea what delights you have missed out upon.'

'Shut up!' she choked. He was twisting the truth around to suit his own version of what he believed and she felt so hurt that she actually began to shake from head to toe in response.

Those unremitting eyes held her captive, and his hand gave a tug to bring her hard up against his solid frame. 'I still cannot look at your mouth without remembering how it feels to have it fixed on some intimate part of my anatomy,' he murmured, his deep voice pulsing inside her head. 'I remember each brush of your lips, each sensuous flick of your sexy tongue. There,' he said huskily. 'Does it make you feel better to know that I am still as obsessed with you as you are with me, Shannon, hmm?'

'I am not obsessed with you—I despise you!' she hissed. 'Or am I supposed to have forgotten the way you slaked yourself in me *after* you alleged my so-called other lover had been there before you, or the way that you slid out of my body still heaving from the whole wild experience only to turn on me like an animal? You spat names at me that I wouldn't call any woman!'

His face went white, and her heart was pounding, not with desire but with a rage two long years in the festering that was suddenly blazing hotly inside.

'I apologised,' he bit back.

Did he really? Well, it can't have been such a sincere apology because she couldn't even bring it to mind! 'What you did to me went beyond apologies,' she told him. 'And do you know what made it worse? You didn't care about me enough to listen to what I had to say before you dealt out your punishment. I was judged and found guilty without even the right to a fair trial! Well, I'll tell you something...' Her breasts were heaving, the words shooting from her on the crest of her rage. 'I will let you right off the hook if you like—because I accept the blame. I did it. I took another man to *your* bed, Luca, and I can't tell you how very much I enjoyed the experience!'

'That's enough!' he barked.

He was right and it was. On a sickening wave of dismay Shannon tugged her wrist free from his grasp and reeled dizzily away. She'd spoken lies—all lies. Why had she done that? she asked herself painfully. Why did she always have to tell him what he wanted to hear?

Behind her the silence was throbbing like the heavy beat of a drum. Inside she was quietly tearing apart at the seams. In her heart she was weeping at all the bitterness, and in her head she was feeling so ugly she never wanted to look at herself again.

'Do I win my pass out of here now?' she asked with a dullness that saw off her anger.

For an answer he spun on his heel and strode away.

Shannon wilted on a combination of shocked horror at what they had thrown at each other and a sinking sense of relief because she had finally driven him to let her out of here. Pulling herself together, she went to gather up her bags, then took in a deep breath before following him.

The moment she stepped back into the kitchen she knew she had not won anything. Luca was playing the domesticated man again and filling the kettle. His overcoat had gone, and his jacket and tie. As she stood there her eyes couldn't resist following the ripple of muscle across broad, tense shoulders.

'Take your coat off, dump the luggage,' he said without turning.

'Luca—for goodness' sake…' she pleaded yet again. 'Just let me out of here so I can find a hotel room somewhere.'

'Tea or coffee?' was all she got by return.

'Oh,' she groaned, covering her now-throbbing eyes with a trembling hand. 'Can't you understand?' she cried in a last-ditch attempt to make him see reason. 'I just can't stay in this apartment with you!'

It was no use. The rigid stretch of cotton barely flexed in response as he stood there waiting for the kettle to boil. 'You're nothing but an unfeeling monster,' she told him as her weary body gave up on the whole stupid fight.

'Tea or coffee,' he repeated.

'Oh, choose which you like,' she sighed, and on an act of surrender sank into one of the chairs at the kitchen table, dropped her bags to the floor, then placed her elbows on the table so she could bury her face in her hands.

Another silence rained down around them after that, broken only by the soothing hiss of the kettle as it came to the boil. Shannon kept her face hidden and Luca—well, she was aware that he was standing there, leaning against the worktop and looking at her, but—what the heck? Let him get his fill of her defeat if that was how he got his kicks these days. She didn't care any more, didn't care about anything but getting a warm drink inside then finding a bed she could sleep in.

Observing the weary way she was sitting there with her face buried in her hands, Luca bit his teeth together and angrily asked himself what the hell he'd thought he was doing orchestrating that little scene. Since when did a reasonably sophisticated man of thirty-four taunt an ex-lover with the kind of remarks he had just poured out?

One that needed an escape for all the burning grief that was trampling his insides, he acknowledged heavily.

And Shannon was not just an ex-lover. She was the woman he'd loved. The woman he'd believed he could spend the rest of his life with. Walking into his own home and seeing what he had seen was going to burn in his head for ever.

'I never did manage to discover who the other man was.'

'What—?' Her face came out of her hands, red-rimmed

eyes staring at him as if he had just spoken to her in Greek. 'It makes you a sad kind of man that you even bothered to try,' she threw back in derision. 'Forget the tea,' she added, dragging herself to her feet again. 'I'll just take the bedroom.'

With that she hauled up her luggage and walked out of the kitchen.

Luca let her go, angry with himself for saying something else he had not meant to say. He stood there listening to her footsteps taking her down the hallway, listened to a door being opened, and a grim smile touched the corners of his mouth because he'd recognised the door as belonging to what she believed was one of the guest bedrooms. She'd picked it out deliberately knowing that their old bedroom was at the other end of the hall.

Standing there tense, hands braced on the worktop, he waited for her to realise the mistake she'd made. Sure enough a few seconds later the door closed and her footsteps continued to the room next door. He hadn't slept in their old bedroom since the day she'd taken another man to it. He would have walked out of the apartment and never come back if it hadn't been too big a step for his pride.

A few seconds later and the next door she had chosen shut with a telling slam. Only then did he let the air leave his body.

He must be mad—crazy to continue to let her get to him like this. What had gone should be forgotten. He wanted to forget, so why was he standing here feeling as bad as he'd felt two years ago?

He knew the answer but hell would freeze over before he would admit it.

The kettle boiled. He watched it happen. Watched it switch off and still remained standing there until the steam had died away again. Then, on a growl of frustration that sounded alien even to him, he turned and followed Shannon's lead by slamming into his own bedroom.

From now on he was going to keep his distance, he vowed grimly. Tomorrow she moved to a hotel. And if they met up again while she was here in Florence then it would be by mistake because he didn't want it to happen.

With that decision made, he stripped off his clothes then strode into the adjoining bathroom, switched on the shower and stepped beneath it. The jet was powerful, the water hot, and as it sluiced down over him he couldn't help but notice what was happening in his lower regions. It made him want to push his fist through the tiled wall in front of him because if Shannon was the only woman who could excite this kind of response in him, then she was right and he was the saddest kind of person indeed.

Shannon opened her suitcase and dragged out a pair of pyjamas, then just stood holding the pale blue strips of flimsy silk in fingers that shook. She despised him, she really did—so why were there tears in her eyes? Why was she feeling so unbelievably hurt because he'd dared to remark on something that should no longer matter to either of them?

If she'd been guilty as charged she might have had reason to feel this wretched. Innocence should bring with it a smug sense of self-righteousness. Only it didn't. Instead it made her want to go and find him, tell the truth and just get it all over with so she could feel comfortable again.

What truth, though? The full truth, warts and all, and other people's secrets? She had tried offering him that truth two years ago only to be scalded by angry disbelief. As far as Luca was concerned she had been caught red-handed trying to tidy away the evidence of another man's recent presence in their bedroom. The rumpled bed had spoken volumes. The packet of condoms had said even more. The fact that she'd dared to try and pass the blame onto someone else had been her final crime in his eyes.

If love had to be tried by such painful methods, then their love was certainly judged that day and found to be utterly wanting in both strength and substance.

And the quicker she got herself out of his orbit, the better it was going to be for both of them, because it was as clear as the nose on her face that he wasn't handling this situation any better than she was.

'Oh, Keira,' she sighed. Just wake up and get well so that I can leave here as quickly as the first flight to London can take me.

Then she thought of Angelo, who had not been given the chance to get well.

Dead.

Her eyes burned. It just wasn't fair. She loved him—everyone loved Angelo. He was that kind of wonderful man.

But no one loved him more than Luca did, she thought painfully. And suddenly she realised she had her reason as to why his behaviour had been so insane.

Remorse raked through her for not realising it earlier. Sympathy followed, along with an aching urge to go and comfort him.

Then she shook on a weary, weary sigh, knowing that the last thing Luca wanted from her was sympathy.

Sex—yes. He'd take the sex as a form of panacea. He'd made that fact only too clear!

On that thought she laid the pyjamas on the bed, removed her clothes, then walked into the adjoining bathroom to step into the shower. The first thing she heard was the sound of water running in the next-door bathroom. It conjured up an image of the naked man in all his god-like proportions, his broad, tanned shoulders, the long golden torso, and the kind of legs built to grip a woman—hard. Her body heated, her breasts grew tight.

Turning on the shower, she forced herself to grimly ignore what was happening on the other side of the wall.

It was bliss to crawl between the cool sheets and put her head down on the pillow, bliss to pull the duvet up to her ears and shut out the rest of the world. Tomorrow I leave here and book into a hotel, was the last thought she remembered having before she dropped like a stone into sleep.

CHAPTER FOUR

CRAMP. Shannon knew what it was even as it brought her screaming out of a deep dark pit of exhaustion. She writhed on the bed, kicking back the covers as her hand shot down to cover the ugly knot that had appeared in her left calf. She groaned and began rubbing at the distressed muscle with the flat of her hand.

It made no difference and if anything only seemed to make her writhe all the more. An agitated need to do something about it before the pain tore her apart sent her agony-bright eyes shooting around the darkened bedroom in search of help from something—anything!

But then her cramping muscle twisted a little tighter and she tumbled off the side of the bed to land in a heap on hard, polished wood squirming and whimpering like a wounded animal.

She had never suffered from cramp in her life before, so she had no idea what to do to ease it. She tried shaking the offending leg, then rubbing it again when the shaking did nothing but make her teeth sing. In sheer desperation she tried to stand up on the dizzy idea that if she could manage to reach the bathroom she could apply something warm to the muscle in the hope heat would help release the angry spasm. But she never made it because the moment she placed any weight on the leg the pain became so unbearable that she landed back on the floor amidst a shrill and shaken cry.

The bedroom door suddenly flew open, and light from the hallway poured into the room. 'What the hell—?' a harsh voice demanded.

Luca stood there. She stared helplessly up at his lean, dark bulk silhouetted against the light. 'Cramp,' she groaned.

It was all she could manage.

To give him credit he didn't need to be told twice. In a couple of strides he was kneeling beside her and gripping the offending leg with ruthless fingers, then began manipulating the cramped muscle in a way that set her teeth singing again.

'I should have known something like this would happen,' he gritted over her whimpered cries of protest. 'When was the last time you bothered to drink anything? You must be dehydrated, you fool!'

Fool or not, she was beginning to see stars now, tears were streaming down her face. 'It hurts,' she cried over and over and kept hitting the floor with a fist while he kept up his grim manipulation of her leg.

Miraculously, though, his form of torture began to ease the other. Sheer relief from the pain brought her out in a shivering cold sweat. 'Aah!' she gasped out shakily. 'That has to be the worst pain I've ever felt in my life.'

But Luca wasn't listening. His dark face locked with anger, he had twisted to pull the light quilt from the bed and was grimly bundling her shivering body into it. Without a word he gathered her into his arms and stood up to carry her out of the bedroom then down the hall and into the kitchen where he finally dumped her on a chair at the table.

Not quite knowing what had hit her, Shannon sat huddling into the quilt while she stared at him in a state of near shock as he crossed the floor and opened the fridge door. A second later he was placing a clean glass tumbler and a bottle of water down on the table.

'Drink,' he commanded.

In mute obedience Shannon unscrewed the bottle top and—ignoring the glass—drank straight from the bottle. Ice-cold, the water was like nectar to her parched mouth and burning throat. After drinking down half the bottle she slumped back in the chair and closed her eyes while she tried to grapple with what had just happened. Her leg felt as if someone had kicked it; the pain had left her shaken and weak. Her head ached with one of those dull throbs that came with too much stress and she felt so tired she could fall asleep where she was sitting.

A sound beside her forced her eyes to open. Luca was leaning against the table beside her chair staring down at his own bare feet. He looked tired and pale, the long day's strain etched into the hard contours of his face.

'Sorry I woke you,' she mumbled.

'I was not asleep,' he replied, and the way he said it told her that he had been lying there thinking about his brother, loving him, hurting for him, wishing the last twenty-four hours had never been.

Her heart turned over, an aching sympathy curling around it. She wanted to reach out and touch him gently, offer words that might help to ease his grief. But there were no such words and she didn't dare mention Angelo's name because whenever she did Luca went ballistic. It was such a helpless, hollow feeling to know that she was not the person he wanted to confide his feelings in.

She would have been, once upon a time. He used to tell her everything. They would lie in bed with limbs tangled and talk and talk and—

'Drink.'

Her eyelashes fluttered against her cheek-bones, then lifted to find him looking at her. His eyes were dark—dark as ebony, sleepy and sultry, his lashes curved and spiky and just begging her to—

She looked away quickly before the senses she could feel beginning to stir took a dangerous grip. Picking up the bottle, she drank some more, hoping the cold water would cool what was beginning to heat. She didn't want to want Luca. She didn't want to remember things about him that she'd learned years before. He was her past. She'd moved on since then.

And just because he was leaning here wearing only a short, hastily tied robe did not mean she had to conjure up memories of the body beneath the robe. So what if this particular man was built to push the female sex drive into meltdown? Sex was sex. These days she looked for deeper things in a relationship like friendship, caring and respect. One day she might even find a man she felt she could trust enough to give him these things. She hadn't stopped looking because of one bad experience. It was just that she hadn't found him yet.

Lifting the bottle to her lips, she drank again. The only illumination in the room came from the down-lighters that were integral to the wall units. The light barely reached the centrally placed table but what did manage to reach cast a warm, seductive glow. And it was quiet, so quiet she thought she could hear the unsteady beat of Luca's heart.

Or was it her heart that was beating unsteadily?

Of course it was her heart. He was too close and she wished that he weren't. Lifting the bottle again, she kept her eyes carefully averted from him and tried to pretend that they were complete strangers.

But averting her eyes didn't do anything but give her imagination a chance to list every detail about him. The length of his legs, for instance, the power in his golden thighs. The robe he was wearing could cover what it liked without making much difference to her for she knew every inch of him, the shape of each separate vertebra in his long, supple spine. She knew the wonderful feel of his satin skin and the contrasting crisp coils of hair that covered his chest. She knew how firm his stomach was, how taut the muscles were in his lean behind. She could draw a picture of every sleek detail from his long brown toes to even longer fingers.

Oh, stop it! she railed herself as a sensation she knew only too well made her squirm. Move away from me! she wanted to yell at him, but instead took another gulp at her drink because saying anything of the kind would be tantamount to confessing what she was thinking and she would rather cut out her tongue than let him know what was inside her head.

A sigh shook her. The kind of sigh that was supposed to ease tension, not help to intensify it—yet that was exactly what this particular sigh did. It intensified everything she was thinking and feeling until the atmosphere began to sing. She wanted to run but remained glued to her seat. She wished those legs weren't right in her field of vision, yet couldn't make herself look the other way.

'What time is it?' she asked with a touch of desperation.

'Three-thirty,' he supplied and even his voice worked its own kind of magic on what was happening to her. It was low and deep and dark and gorgeously accented. It tugged at her heartstrings, which in turn tugged at more susceptible things.

She ached on a silent groan. Will I ever get over him? The first love syndrome, she thought helplessly. They say that you never really recover from your first true love.

'How is the muscle?'

Like a wooden puppet, she put a hand down to rub the offending calf. It still felt tight but it was no longer knotting.

'OK,' she replied and drank some more water. It came as a shock to realise that somewhere in the last few minutes he had exchanged her empty bottle for a full one. 'How many of these do you want me to drink before you'll let me go back to bed?'

It was said in an effort to lighten the tension, and he

dutifully laughed. But the low sound only set her flesh tingling. 'Keep going until I tell you to stop,' he replied.

Then the silence came back. Her pulse began to race, the previously even rhythm of her breathing shattering so badly that she shifted restlessly on the chair in an effort to contain it all. The action made one of the thin straps of her flimsy top slide off her shoulder. Finding herself in real danger of exposing a tightly thrusting nipple, she reached up to tug the offending strap back into place again—only to clash with long brown fingers as they went to do the same thing.

Both of them went absolutely still with fingers resting against fingers, while her flesh began to heat. She glanced up. It was instinctive. What she saw sent her heart-rate into overdrive.

He was looking at her body. His dark eyes were hidden beneath those spiky black lashes as they grazed over a smooth white shoulder, then dipped lower to the rounded slopes of her breasts.

He wanted to touch her.

'No,' she breathed in shaky rejection and made a clumsy grab at the slipping duvet.

Her denial brought his lashes up. Black heat from his eyes shot towards her and held her trapped in a dark, dark mesh. The duvet remained where it was, lying in a soft, squashy heap on her lap and the sting of desire leapt through her blood, tripping sensual switches as it went.

He knew—he knew. Everything about him was turning dark on the knowledge. Dark eyes, dark heart, a searing dark ardour that coiled itself around the both of them. Nothing about him was light any more, or gentle or soft. He wanted her but didn't want to want her. She returned the resentful feeling.

His fingers began to trail across her shoulder. Moving with a tantalising slowness until they reached the long column of her neck, then slid sideways, combing her tangled hair away from her nape. Shannon stopped breathing. Luca did the opposite. Pulling a deep, hard breath of air into his lungs, he moved, dipping his dark head to fasten white teeth on the creamy flesh he had just exposed.

Sensation shot through her like a thousand pinpricks; she gasped and quivered, then stroked her cheek against his face. Animal, they were animals, she the purring preening she-cat responding to her demanding mate. His hands slid beneath her arms and lifted her onto her feet. His mouth moved from nape to her mouth and she stood on one foot, favouring her cramped leg as she sank herself into the all-consuming heat of his kiss.

What had been threatening to spark between them from the moment they'd first faced each other across the threshold of her London flat now flared up with spectacular energy. They kissed as they used to kiss, long and deep and holding back nothing. Her arms went around his neck; the duvet lay around her feet. He moved his hands down her slender sides, moulding her fine-boned feminine shape, then gripping her waist to draw her between his legs. He was still leaning against the table but the robe had slid apart at his waist. She felt the heat of him, the powerful thrust of his sex against her stomach, and knew that she was not going to be the one to stop this.

Would he stop it? She moaned against his mouth in horror of it happening. He took the groan to mean something else.

'No way,' he muttered, and explained his meaning by shifting his hands again. Her pyjama bottoms slithered downwards to come to rest at her knees. She accepted the force of his thrust between her thighs and held him there while the kiss went on and on and her pyjama top was eased away from her breasts. He touched, she went wild for him. Her fingers clutched at his hair and her thighs tightened their possessive grip. On a dark growl he picked her up and began walking without allowing the kiss to break until he let go of her and she landed in the middle of a rumpled bed.

For a horrible moment she thought he was going to turn and walk away. It would be just punishment in his eyes, she knew that. But, far from walking away, Luca stripped off his robe and came to join her, ridding her of the flimsy scraps of blue silk before sliding his powerful frame over the top of hers and returning his mouth to hers.

They kissed right through the whole tempestuous journey. Not once did either of them attempt to break free. They touched with hands and the sensual shift of their bodies; when they needed more he penetrated her with a single silken thrust. She cried out against his mouth; he answered the cry with a grunt that raked the back of his throat. Her fingers had a tight grip on his hair again, her legs were wrapped around him, like two tight clamps. He moved to a primitive rhythm, his chest rasping against her breasts.

Animal? Yes, it was animal. A hungry coupling of two wild creatures that did not want to think about the past or the present or even the future. They just wanted—*needed* this.

This came with a power to make her lose contact with reality. Gasps, groans and shudders arrived in unison. Mingled sweat and body-heat and, finally, body fluids that left them wasted and eventually shocked.

He got up the moment he was physically able. Snatching up his robe, he slammed out of the room. Shannon watched him go with her heart in her eyes, then curled into a ball and sobbed her heart out.

He hated her—despised himself for touching her at all.

When daylight came, she opened her eyes to a pale sun seeping through the window and with her body aching like mad and her heart locked into a dull throb. She continued to lie there for a while, reluctant to move when moving meant having to face Luca.

Then she remembered Keira, and was grimly pushing Luca to one side and hurrying into the bathroom.

Choosing the first things out of her case that came to hand, she pulled on her jeans and added a clean blue top, then repacked the case. She wasn't staying here another night.

As she opened the bedroom door the seductive aroma of fresh coffee teased her senses, the thought that Luca was up and about made those same senses squirm. She didn't want to see him. If she could get away from here without having to face him she would do.

She never wanted to have to set eyes on him again.

But there he stood, looking very sombre and civilised in beautifully cut black silk trousers and a crisp white shirt. He was standing by a kitchen unit playing the domestic again. Her stomach dipped; she followed it by placing her bags down by the kitchen door.

'Sit down,' he invited. 'This won't be a minute.' He indicated the large pot of coffee brewing beside him.

But he didn't turn to look at her as he said it, which spoke volumes to her. Too ashamed of himself? If so, he wasn't the only one to feel that way.

'Did you ring the hospital?' she asked him stiffly.

He nodded. 'There is still no change,' he supplied.

'Then I would rather be going.'

'After we have eaten,' he came back uncompromisingly. 'I don't think either of us got around to eating much yesterday.'

We ate each other, Shannon thought bitterly. 'I don't—'

'We played this scene in your kitchen, Shannon,' he cut in. 'I see no use in doing it again.'

In other words, shut up. Pressing her lips together, she moved to the table and sat herself down. If he sticks toast under my nose I shall probably throw it back at him, she decided mutinously. Then felt a wave of panic wash over her when he turned suddenly as if she'd said the words out loud.

Not that she was afraid of him—only his expression. She preferred to keep looking at his back. In fact she would prefer it a lot more if she did not have to look at him at all. So she kept her eyes lowered as he crossed to the table, and placed the coffee pot before her.

Then he went still because he'd noticed her bag standing by the door and a new tension began to suck the oxygen out of the air. He was going to say something about last night, she was sure of it. If he did she was out of here even if that meant jumping down the lift shaft.

'About last night…'

She shot to her feet like a bullet.

'I want to apologise for—'

She moved on trembling legs towards the door.

'Shannon…'

'No!' She swung on him furiously. 'Don't you dare start telling me how much you regret it! Don't you dare, do you hear me, Luca? Don't you *dare*!'

'I hear you,' he said very quietly.

She looked at him then, really looked at him and saw exactly what she'd expected to see—his handsome dark features locked into a cold stone wall of self-contempt and regret. A sob caught in her throat. She wanted to hide her shame. She wanted the ground to open up and swallow her whole!

'Keira has to be all that matters here,' she pushed out unsteadily. 'You—m-me—*we* don't matter. I won't let you force me into running away this time!'

'I don't want you to run,' he sighed out irritably.

The question— Then what do you want from me?—sang in a silence that hung.

She didn't ask it. Instead she lifted trembling fingers to her mouth, tried to swallow, then lowered them again.

'I have to move to a hotel—today,' she told him.

There was a movement of tight male muscle, a flash of black fury hitting his eyes. 'And I have to claim my brother's body today!' he lashed at her harshly. 'What do you think is more important right now?'

She took a jerky step backwards, shaken to her roots by what he'd said. 'I'm so sorry,' she whispered painfully 'I didn't know!'

'I know that,' he snapped, still frowning blackly as he swung away again. 'We are both having to deal with an intolerable situation,' he said tightly. 'Needs cross, emotions get out of control. It has to be expected that our priorities will clash.'

Wise words, she acknowledged, if she was able to ignore the fact that she had been so wrapped up in her own grievances and distress she'd allowed herself to forget all of his.

And what were her grievances? she asked herself. So, they'd done the unforgivable last night but both had been guilty of falling into that particular dark pit, greedily assuaging one set of emotions, then overwhelming them with a different set.

Because Luca had pulled away from her afterwards did not mean she could shift all the blame onto him. In fact, while she was being brutally honest here—if he hadn't pulled away, then she probably would have.

The new silence gnawed at the tension in the atmosphere. She wished she could say something to make them both feel better but she couldn't think what. He was standing there wearing a rod of iron strapped across his broad shoulders, and his fingers were gripping the worktop with enough power to put dents in to the solid black marble.

'Sit down again,' he gritted.

Sit down, she repeated to herself, and looked down at the way her bags were standing at her feet like a childish defiance. Without saying a word she picked them up, turned and left the kitchen. Walking down the hall, she went back into the bedroom, put the bags down by the bed then walked back the way she had come. Fingers fluttered momentarily, coinciding with the deep, shaky breath she took before she pushed open the kitchen door and stepped back in.

Luca was still standing where she had left him, long brown fingers still gripping the worktop like a vice. She wanted to go to him, put her arms around him and *show* him just how badly she felt for forgetting what really mattered. But instead she crossed to the table and sat down.

And the silence pulsed in her eardrums, it throbbed in her stomach and pulled at the flesh covering her face. *Move*! She wanted to shout at him. *Say* something—*anything*! I've said I'm sorry. I've made the climb down. I don't know what else to do!

Maybe he tapped into her thought patterns—he'd always been able to do that. He turned, walked towards the table. The predicted rack of toast was set down in front of her.

'I will organise a hotel suite for you,' he announced curtly, then left her alone to swallow the unpalatable fact that her climb down had been a complete waste of time.

An hour later and she was at her sister's bedside, delivered there by Luca who, once he'd checked on Keira, left again, his lean face scored by the grim task that lay ahead of him, one that would to strip his self-control to the bone.

Tears for them all flooded her eyes as she sat gently stroking Keira's soft brown hair. She and her sister were so unalike in so many ways, she thought fondly. The colour of their hair, for instance, and the differences in character. Where she was bright and independent and naturally self-confident, Keira had always been shy and unsure of herself. Meeting and falling in love with Angelo had put stars in her eyes and an anxious pallor on her soft cheeks. She could never quite believe that a dashingly handsome man like Angelo could fall in love with a timid little mouse like her.

So she'd worked hard all her marriage to make herself feel worthy of her man. It had infuriated Shannon to watch it sometimes. 'You spoil him too much. He'll start treating you like a doormat if you don't watch out.'

But Angelo had remained faithfully besotted to his Irish mouse. It was the mouse who'd taken Shannon by surprise by turning into a sly little fox. 'Idiot,' she whispered and was suddenly fighting a battle with fresh tears again.

What followed was a long and hard nerve-flaying day in which Shannon divided her time between Keira and the nursery.

By two o'clock she was beginning to feel drained of emotional energy and was actually glad to be given some respite from her bedside vigil when a team of medical staff appeared and she was ushered away.

She needed some air that did not smell of the hospital. So she bought a sandwich in the downstairs cafeteria and took it with her to eat outside. The sun was bright and the air was cool, fresh—clean. Walking through the neatly laid gardens, she found a bench in the sunshine and sat down, unwrapped her sandwich and tried to empty all thoughts from her head so that she could attempt to eat at least.

Luca tracked her down ten minutes later. Her hair was up scrunched into a twist of narrow black ribbon, and the curve of her slender neck looked disturbingly vulnerable to him. The thought made him grimace because he wasn't thinking of vulnerable as in fragile, he was thinking vulnerable as in ripe for tasting. His tongue even moistened at the prospect, and he wished that he didn't have to look at her through the eyes of a recent lover.

But he did. Giving in to his baser instincts might have been a stupid mistake but he was now stuck with the results of it. Last night he had gone a little insane. He had lost control of himself. Two years ago she'd left him, taking his manhood with her when she went. Last night she gave it back to him. He should be pleased. He should be feeling the triumph of retribution and be able to walk away free and whole and ready to get on with the rest of his life, but all he felt was…

Need, greed—it had many names but they all came wrapped up in the same package. He wanted more and no amount of self-aimed contempt was going to change that.

Maybe he should go out and find himself a woman. There were certainly a lot out there more than willing to share his bed. Maybe now that Shannon had released him from his sexual prison he could even do both himself and these other woman some of his old macho justice.

But he didn't want them; he wanted this one. This red-haired, white-skinned, blue eyed betrayer who made his body sing.

A wry smile played with the tired corners of his mouth as he started walking again. The slight tensing in Shannon's shoulders as she'd sensed his approach gave that smile a different edge. Love each other or hate each other, they could still tune into the others presence like wild cats sniffing territorial scent.

Stepping around the bench, he paused for a moment to study the strain in her face. Her hair might burn like fire in the sunlight but her cheeks were pale, her eyes too dark and there was a telling hint of hurt about the way she was holding her mouth.

On a heavy sigh, he remembered why it was that he had come to find her. Slipping free the single button holding his jacket together, he sat down next to her with a long sigh.

'I'm sorry there was no one here with you,' he murmured quietly. 'It has been a—tough morning for everyone, I'm afraid.'

She turned to look at him, expression guarded as she looked into his face. He was beginning to look haggard, he knew, and did not bother to hide it. 'I thought it was tough enough five years ago when we had to do this for my father but…' He stopped, mouth tightening on words he didn't want to say but knew in the end that he had no choice. 'My mother collapsed and has had to be sedated. Renata is finding it difficult to cope. Sophia offered to come here to sit with you but she is needed by Mama.'

'I understand,' she returned.

'Do you?' Luca wished that he did. It felt as if the whole family had been involved in that car crash—himself and Shannon included. 'It's a mess,' he muttered and leaned forward to rest his forearms on his knees, his throat working on the now-permanent lump stuck in it. 'I've got people dropping like flies all around me. Formalities to deal with. A company that refuses to stop running just because I want it to. The phones keep on ringing. We are sinking beneath a wave of sympathy that, to be honest, I could do without right now.' His voice was growing husky—he could hear it.

Would she scream abuse at him if he also admitted that he wanted to pick her up and carry her off to the nearest bed to lose himself in her for an hour or two?

'The thing is, Shannon, I need to ask a big favour…'

She tensed. He grimaced as his mind made a connection with what he'd been thinking and what he'd just said. But, of course, Shannon didn't know about that.

'I need to be sure you are OK, you see,' he went on. 'Thinking of you alone in some faceless hotel room when you are not here does not make me feel OK.' He turned his head to look at her. The sunlight was trying its best to put some colour onto her drawn cheeks but it wasn't succeeding, and her mouth looked so vulnerable he wanted to—

'So I would like to take back my offer to find you somewhere else to stay. I want you to go on living at my place. I will move out if you prefer,' he offered, watching her carefully for some kind of reaction, but he wasn't getting one. 'But I would rather stay there too. That way I will know you will not be on your own if the—'

'Don't say it,' she said.

'No,' he agreed, looking down at his long fingered hands hanging limp between his spread knees.

While Shannon looked at the top of his dark head, watching the sun gloss it with a silken sheen. If the worst happens during the night, was what he had been going to say. Having shared her time between Keira and the baby, she was more than aware that the 'worst' wasn't very far away. As she watched the baby grow stronger with every passing hour she watched the baby's mama slowly fade.

'About last night,' he inserted suddenly.

Shannon sucked in a sharp breath. His hands moved, flexing tensely before pleating together, and she saw a nerve at the edge of his jaw give a jerk.

'I went a little crazy,' he admitted. 'I am ashamed of myself for taking my—feelings out on you.'

'We both went a little crazy.' She shifted tensely.

'It won't happen again,' he promised.

'No,' she agreed.

'So will you stay at my apartment?'

She looked down at her lap where the remains of her half-eaten sandwich lay slotted in its triangular casing and watched it blur out of focus on the onset of tears. 'Keira isn't ever going to wake up, is she?' she whispered.

Luca didn't answer for a moment, then he shook his dark head. 'I don't think so,' he responded huskily.

'I'll stay,' she agreed on a thick swallow.

Luca sat back against the bench suddenly and the air hissed out from between his teeth in a tense, taut act of relief. A moment later something dropped on her lap next to the sandwich carton.

It was a plastic security card. 'Access,' he explained. 'You might need it if I cannot get here to collect you.'

She nodded.

'If I cannot make it then my driver Fredo will come for you. You remember Fredo?'

'Yes.' Another nod while she stared down at the card. Fredo was a wiry little man with amazing patience—he needed it for the hours he tended to hang around waiting for Luca to appear.

'Good,' he said. 'Then I don't have to worry about you getting into the back of some stranger's car.'

It was a joke. She hadn't expected it. It surprised her enough to force a small laugh out of her. Luca laughed too, one of those deep, soft, husky sounds of his that caressed the senses. But it all felt so strange and wrong to be laughing in the circumstances that soon they both fell silent and still.

'You don't have to worry about me at all,' she thrust into that stillness.

'Worry is not the word that shoots into my head,' he countered. 'Someone should be here with you supporting you through this. Here.' Something else landed on her lap. She stared in surprise at the sight of her own mobile telephone. 'It was in my overcoat pocket. I found it this morning,' Luca explained. 'Here is my private number. Log it in the phone's memory. Don't hesitate to call me if you need me, Shannon.' It was a serious threat more than polite reassurance.

Then he stood up so suddenly that he made her blink. Big and lean and dark and tense, he blocked out her sunlight. She felt cold—bereft. He was going to leave and she wanted to fling herself at him and beg him to stay!

But he had duties to return to and she had a bedside vigil to keep.

'I have to go.' He stated the obvious and tension zipped through the air like electric static. 'Use the phone, do you hear me?'

Shannon pressed her lips hard together and nodded. He

turned and strode away without glancing back and she remained sitting there with the sun trying to put back the warmth he had taken with him.

It didn't.

Luca had never felt so inadequate or useless in his entire life as he did when he walked away from her like that. But he had things to deal with, lousy, throat-locking, soul-stripping *things* that could not be put off.

But his mind was locked into Shannon—or was it his heart? He didn't know. What he did know was that Shannon might have betrayed him two years ago but he was betraying her now by not being there when she needed him.

And it had to be him. That was the other part of his inner conflict that was flaying him alive. He did not want someone else to be there with her. He didn't even want to think about her leaning on someone else.

'*Dio*, leave me in peace!' he rasped when the land-line on the desk began to ring.

It was a reporter wanting him to make a statement. This was not the first insensitive lout he'd had to deal with today and probably would not be the last. As he was replacing the receiver Renata put her head round the door to look him a question. She'd added ten years in twenty-four hours. They all had.

'No,' he said. 'It was the press, not the hospital.'

Renata remained hovering in the doorway and he knew she wanted him to hold her. Walking across the room, he took her in his arms and let her weep into his shoulder and wished it could be OK for him to break down and weep.

'How is Mama?' he asked when the flood subsided.

'She's awake now, and looking a little stronger,' Renata told him, then added carefully. 'Luca, about Shannon—'

'Don't go there, Renata,' he warned thinly and was glad of the excuse to move away from her when the phone rang again. His sister hovered for a few seconds longer, silenced by his censure and waiting to find out who was calling before slipping away once she knew the call was business.

He did not want to discuss the rights and wrongs of Shannon staying with him at his apartment. He did not want to discuss Shannon with anyone—period.

His personal assistant was asking him a question that required his full concentration. Luca gave it to him and dealt with the problem as if it were perfectly normal to make corporate decisions while the world lay in rubble at his feet.

It was while he was in the middle of a curt, clipped sentence that his private cell-phone began to beep.

Shannon. He was certain of it. He dropped the other phone as if it were a hot brick.

His fingers shook as he made the connection. All she could manage to say to him was, 'Please—will you come?'

CHAPTER FIVE

LUCA came to a stop in the doorway, a thick breath labouring in his chest. He was too late. She had called him too late. Now he was having to stand here and witness just how alone she must have felt.

The doctors had advised him to take her away now, but how did you prize those slender white fingers from her beautiful, beautiful sister's fingers for the last time?

Tears hit his eyes and remained there, burning like acid, though he did not let them fall. It was going to happen soon, he knew that. Soon he was going to give way to all of this hard, aching grief and cry himself empty, he promised himself.

But for now he wanted to hit something again, put his fist through a window or a wall. The pain it would cause had to be more bearable than what he was suffering right now, he thought grimly as he made himself walk forward on legs that felt hollow and slowly went down on his haunches next to Shannon's chair. She didn't even notice, but as he gathered up her free hand her eyelashes flickered and she looked at him.

'It's over,' she whispered.

'*Sì,*' he murmured unevenly. 'I know.'

Her eyes drifted back to her sister's quietly serene face and she forgot he was there again for a while, then the sound of a muffled sob came from somewhere behind them, and glancing round Luca saw that the rest of his family had arrived.

He'd taken off without them with Fredo driving like a madman leaving the others to find their own way here, now they poured forward, crowding the bed to begin this next wave of unbearable grief. As they pressed around the bed he saw Shannon become aware, blinking blank and dazed eyes at the sudden commotion, and he knew by instinct that she was not going to cope with the Italian way of letting feelings pour out like this.

With his jaw set like a closed vice, he reached across for her other hand and with gentle fingers began carefully easing it away from Keira's hand.

Shannon gasped and looked him a pained protest. But he shook his head. 'It's time to let go, *cara*,' he told her gently.

For a moment he thought she was going to refuse. She looked back at her sister with glistening tears drawing a film across her eyes and it ripped him apart inside because he knew those tears displayed the beginning of acceptance.

A few seconds after that she allowed him to complete the separation, allowed him to ease his arm around her waist and help her to her feet. The others flooded towards her now, crowding her by reaching out to embrace her and murmuring their tearful phrases of condolence; his mother looking dreadful, his weeping sisters and their sober-faced husbands all taking their turn.

Shannon accepted their embraces from within a cocoon of dazed bewilderment and clung tightly to one of Luca's hands.

Keira was gone.

Angelo and Keira. Was it all right for her to use their names together like that now? She looked up at Luca standing big and dark like a guard beside her; his handsome face was locked up again, mouth grim, eyes hot. It wasn't the face to which you asked such a question, she thought, and allowed him to guide her towards the door, leaving her sister surrounded by people who'd always loved her unstintingly.

There was consolation in that somehow.

'The baby,' she said as they reached the quietness of the corridor.

'Not now,' Luca said and kept her moving—away towards the lifts, then down and across the ground floor foyer out into the late afternoon sunlight. It was cold and she shivered. She saw Fredo was there looking solemn as he held open the rear door to a big silver car. Luca guided her inside, then followed. Almost as soon as the door closed behind him he was reaching for her and drawing her into his arms.

They stayed like that for the time it took Fredo to deliver them to the apartment, Shannon leaning limply against him, lost somewhere inside the mists of shock while he gave her what he instinctively knew she needed—his silent strength.

He continued to hold her close as they walked across the main foyer of the apartment block; he kept her wrapped in his arms as they rode the lift. When they reached the apartment she suddenly broke free and headed straight for her bedroom. Luca needed to use a few moments to put a clamp on what was threatening to break loose from inside him, then he followed with the intention of making sure she was all right before he left her alone to her grief.

But it did not work out like that. One glance at her lying curled on her side in the middle of the bed and he was kicking off his shoes, dragging off his jacket and tie, then joining her.

It was really quite pathetic the way she accepted his arms as they drew her in, and near impossible not to shed tears with her when she began to weep quietly.

When she eventually went silent he reached beneath and tugged out the duvet, then covered them both.

'I don't—' she went to protest.

'You are so cold you're shivering,' he cut in huskily. 'Stay here with me like this for a little while,' he encouraged. 'Once you warm up a bit I will go and leave you in peace.'

'I don't want you to go.' It was so soft and weak he almost missed it. But he didn't miss the way her fingers drifted across his shirt front and settled in a tremulous curl around his nape. Her breath feathered along his jawline, her breasts felt soft against his ribs and a slender leg slid across his thighs as she pressed herself closer as if it was the only place she wanted to be. He closed his eyes and wished it did not feel so good to be needed by her like this.

That need continued through the ensuing dark days when Shannon was aware of very little if Luca was not there to make her.

'Eat,' he'd say and she would eat. 'Sleep,' and she would curl up in her bed like a child and close her eyes obediently.

In the mornings they would share breakfast, then Luca would drive her to the hospital to be with the baby while he went off to attend to—other things. In the afternoon he would arrive back at the hospital to spend a little time in the nursery before taking Shannon back to his apartment to ply her with more food and make her talk about work, her life in London, Keira and Angelo—about anything so long as she was made to use her brain.

She moved around as if surrounded by a fog, though she didn't mind. It might be cold but it was oddly comforting—she liked it. The Salvatore family were being kind to her. They had managed to put their resentments aside in these days of a shared grief. Mrs Salvatore invited her to come and stay with her, but Shannon declined. 'I want to stay with Luca,' she explained, too lost in her fog to see that the invitation had been issued to get her *away* from Luca. But it would not have mattered if she had been aware of it because Luca himself happened to overhear the invitation, and turned it down.

The only time the fog cleared was when she was with the

baby. In fact her world began to revolve around the tiny and sweet, tragically orphaned daughter of Angelo and Keira.

Having had personal experience, Shannon knew exactly how it felt to be orphaned at birth. She and Keira had been brought up by a spinster aunt who'd come to Dublin and carried the two girls off to live with her in England. Shannon knew all of this because Keira had told her. Only three years older than herself, yet Keira had remembered it all so vividly. Maybe it was Aunt Merrill's no-nonsense efficiency at that time that had turned the frightened and bewildered Keira, who was missing her mother, into such a timid mouse, whereas Shannon had never known anything else but Aunt Merrill's no-nonsense, 'I don't have time to deal with this' attitude, so she'd learned to be independent very young.

Aunt Merrill shocked everyone by marrying and moving to live with her new husband in South America only weeks after Keira's wedding and while Shannon was in her first term at university. It had not occurred to either sister that the woman they'd sort of relied upon had been chafing at the bit waiting for the moment when her responsibility towards them would finish so that she could get on with her own life. Neither of them had resented their aunt for doing that, but with Keira living in Florence and busy building her marriage, Shannon had been left alone to fend for herself while she'd finished her education. What emerged from those years of self-sufficiency was a bright and super-confident young woman brimming with a zest for life.

Her aunt knew what had happened to Keira and Angelo because Shannon had rung her up to break the news. Merrill offered her sympathy but said she would not be able to attend the funerals because she had too many commitments. When Aunt Merrill had fulfilled her commitments to her sister's children she'd well and truly cut them out of her life.

Looking down at the small baby she held cradled in her arms, 'It will never be like that between you and me,' she vowed softly. 'You, my precious, will have my lifelong love.'

Luca appeared, striding into the nursery like a dynamic force wearing one of the sombre dark suits she'd grown used to seeing him in over the last week. He looked tired, drained to the dregs of his energy by too much heartache and too many painful, emotion-stripping formalities to deal with. But his face softened into a smile when he saw Shannon cradling the small pink bundle in her arms.

'She's been unplugged,' he exclaimed in soft surprise as he came down on his haunches to brush a gentle finger along the baby's pink cheek.

'Half an hour ago.' Shannon smiled too. 'They just came in and took out the leads and tubes and handed her to me.'

'May I take her?' he requested, and without hesitation he received the tiny person into the crook of his arm.

Straightening up, Luca strolled away to the window, his dark head bowed as he gazed down at his brother's child. She was exquisite. A tiny pink rosebud Angelo would have fallen instantly in love with.

Well, I've done it for him, he thought adoringly. Angelo's daughter was never going to feel the loss of her father's love, he vowed, and lowered his head to seal the vow with the light brush of his lips to her petal-soft cheek.

'I must formally register her birth soon,' he remarked as one thought led him onwards. He'd become quite the expert on the official procedures required for registering birth and death, he mused. 'This little angel needs a name.'

'She already has one,' Shannon said, then flushed when he lifted his eyes to send her a sardonically questioning glance.

‘Well, this is interesting,’ he drawled, and he glanced back at the baby. ‘It seems you have a name no one else knows about, *mia dolce piccola*. Perhaps your Aunt Shannon would like to share it with us?’

Aunt Shannon suddenly looked distinctly defensive. ‘I call her Rose,’ she murmured. ‘It—it’s Keira’s middle name.’

‘I know it is,’ Luca said quietly. ‘I was merely wondering if there was a second or two when you considered giving all of us an opportunity to offer up our own suggestions…?’

He could see by the frown pulling at her brow that there had not been a second when she had considered such a thing. ‘I haven’t gone over your head and made it official. It’s just *my* name for her,’ she then said uncomfortably. ‘If you have any objections then just—’

‘I like it,’ he cut in, making that point clear, though his eyes narrowed slightly as a sudden suspicion began to play with his head.

If Shannon had decided on the baby’s name without consulting with anyone else, could it be that she was harbouring ideas of possession that did not include anyone else?

He studied her tired face with its blue eyes set in saddened darkness and the downward turn that had taken virtual permanent control of her beautiful mouth. Her skin looked so delicate it reminded him of finely stretched silk—touch it and it would tear apart.

His gaze drifted lower, moving over the black jeans that made her legs look more slender than ever and the navy blue top that hid nothing he couldn’t picture for himself. She barely ate and it was showing. She barely slept—though he was aware that she did not know he listened to her as she paced his apartment in the dead of night. She was beautiful but bruised, beautiful but lost in her own world of grief that shut out everyone else.

But he had plans for this baby. He had plans for her aunt. Aware though that this was not the time to voice those plans, he continued amiably, 'If I could make a small addition—for my mother's sake, you understand. We could name her Rosita, use Rose as our name for her and add Angelina, in Angelo's memory—what do you think?'

Shannon thought it sounded so beautifully appropriate that it brought the ready tears to her eyes. 'Yes, I would like that,' she whispered and was too lost in thoughts of Angelo and Keira to notice how the baby girl had just become fully Italian.

'Here…' Luca said, and gave her back the baby, watched the tears drift away to be replaced with a loving smile and was quietly satisfied with the smooth way he had handled this. 'Say your farewell, then we must be going…'

They had the ordeal of a double funeral to get through tomorrow and Shannon needed something to wear. She knew this because they had discussed it over breakfast this morning and she had reluctantly agreed to let him take her shopping. But by the scowling expression she sent him he knew she had changed her mind.

'No way,' he firmly vetoed the look. 'You need the break from here and a change of scenery—*I* need the same. You never know,' he added lightly as she stood up and without comment went to lay the baby down in her cot. 'We might even catch ourselves enjoying it.'

Oddly enough they did enjoy themselves. Luca took her back to the apartment for a quick shower before they headed into the city. Shannon changed into the only dress she had brought with her to Florence—a deep sapphire-blue long-sleeved knit thing that clung to her slender figure and highlighted the colour of her eyes. She applied some make-up for the first time in a week, brushed out her hair and decided on impulse to leave it loose. Slipping her feet into a pair of slender-heeled shoes, she then went to look for Luca—and found him in the sitting room stretched out on one of the brown sofas reading a magazine while waiting for her, just as he used to do.

The familiarity of the pose brought her to a standstill in the doorway. It jolted her right out of her comfortable fog. He looked so achingly beautiful, so long and dark and sleek and so much her kind of man that her heart turned over. When he caught sight of her standing by the door, the sight of his easy smile took away her ability to breathe.

When he tossed the magazine aside to rise lithely to his feet she knew she had got herself into deep trouble here because everything about him was drawing her to him, like that old magnetic pull they used to share. He'd changed his suit for casual dark grey trousers and a soft black leather jacket worn over a wine-red shirt. In sharp suits he was expensive and dynamic; in casual clothes he became—dangerous.

And now he had gone still—other than for slumber-dark eyes, which were roaming over her as if he too were only just seeing her for the first time this week.

'Quite an exquisite transformation,' he murmured softly, and began walking towards her.

Shannon watched him come through guarded eyes because she knew what he was thinking. He was thinking—mine—sex—I want. She recognised the sensually possessive gleam. Her stomach muscles gave an agitated tingle, the tips of her breasts stirring in their old electric response to him.

'Beautiful,' he murmured, then bent to touch her mouth with his and maintained the light contact until he felt her lips quiver before he lifted his head again. 'Ready to go?' he enquired with subtle innocence.

Her uncertain nod came with an equally uncertain frown because she knew that kiss had been a deliberate gesture—like a warning foretaste of what was to come.

Did she want what was to come? She didn't know yet—

she didn't even know if she wanted to leave here at all feeling as unsettled and confused as she did.

'Then let's do it,' he said, as if he were answering the questions she was asking of herself.

They drove into the centre of Florence, winding through the back streets until they reach the pedestrian zone where Luca parked the car. It was warmer than it had been since she'd arrived in Italy and the sun was bright so she left her coat in the car and they set out walking.

Luca settled a hand at her waist as if it had every right to be there. The top of her head reached to just above his shoulder; every time he spoke to her he turned to look her deep in her eyes. She could feel herself becoming mesmerised yet couldn't seem to do anything about it. Even though she knew he was deliberately building the intimacy between them, she was just too susceptible to slap him down.

That was the trouble with tragedy and grief, she excused her own weak behaviour—it sapped your strength to fight.

They turned heads as they walked together. It had always been this way for them because they made such a striking contrast—he the tall, dark man of Florence and she the white-skinned slender creature with hair that flamed.

A man stopped to utter something candidly naughty about them to Luca in Italian and when Shannon made the translation she couldn't resist an impulsive laugh. Luca grinned, white-toothed and wicked. The stranger looked momentarily shocked at Shannon's laughing response, then he was grinning as he went on his way leaving them to do the same.

They reached the great *Duomo* cathedral with its gleaming white ribs set against terracotta tiles. As they walked beneath its mighty shadow Shannon did what she knew she had been aching to do and slipped her arm around Luca's lean waist.

Luca didn't want it to stop. He did not want to take her into one of the élite shops on *Via dei Tornabuoni* and snuff out her lingering smile by shrouding her in black mourning clothes. So he diverted them into the elegant café *Giacosa* and ordered cappuccino and pastries, which they shared while he carefully set her talking about her life in London and her graphic design business until she was talking away with all her old zest and enthusiasm, shooting him questions, picking at his brains—and other parts of him, just as she used to do.

It was mad, he knew it. Allowing himself to become bewitched again was a fool's way to go. But he had plans for Shannon and if those plans were a poor excuse for letting her inch her way back into his system then he was ready to fool himself that he was in control.

Shopping in Florence was a serious occupation. No one knew how to shop better than the Italians. They were born with an innate sense of class and unquestionable style. Luca was no different, so it was he that decided on a suit because of the sleek, timeless classicism of its beautiful fabric and wonderful cut. After buying the suit they window-shopped on *Via dei Tornabuoni*, stopping to buy bag and shoes, before moving on to *Via dei Pecori* to select the rest of the things she required. The moment an assistant settled the first black veil on Shannon's head Luca saw the change come over her face and knew she'd remembered why they were doing this, so he distracted her with an extravagant showering of expensive lingerie, which made her blush, then smile.

They took her purchases back to the car, then Luca suggested that they walk down to the river to watch the sun go down. Shannon agreed, aware that he was peeling back the years to a different time when everything was wonderful and they used to do this kind of thing often. Luca was as irresistible as he had been back then. Smiling, talking naturally with him while holding hands as they strolled along the *Lungarni* and onto the *Ponte Santa Trinita* to watch the sunset on the Arno, was like dipping her hand into very hot water—and discovering that she liked it.

'Oh, just look, Luca...' she prompted softly as the river turned into a silk ribbon of fire and warmed the famous face of the *Ponte Vecchio*—the next bridge in the line. 'How do you ever get used to looking at this?'

They were standing shoulder to shoulder against the bridge looking down the river, but he turned at her words to run his gaze over her face tinted golden by the sun and her hair shot with flames. 'I don't,' he said.

Inner flutters took flight in her stomach because she knew he was referring to her, not the view. She glanced at him. 'Now that was corny,' she chided, 'and very un-Italian of you.'

'It is the truth—why pretend?' He shrugged lazily.

She was suddenly racked by a cold shiver as the cool water rising from the river touched her skin. 'I'm cold,' she said and pushed away from the bridge to begin walking back the way they had come, aware that she'd left Luca still leaning there absorbing the change in mood.

He soon caught up with her, though, his leather jacket arriving across her shoulders along with his arm to hold it there. 'Thank you,' she murmured a trifle stiffly.

'Prego,' he drawled with a lightness that told her he was going to ignore the mood change and his arm remained where it was across her shoulders, casual yet intimate and possessive.

'Where shall we eat?' he asked after a moment.

'It's too early for dinner.' For an Italian, anyway.

'You prefer to go back to the apartment now?'

No, she didn't. Going back meant making a decision about what came after they got there and she knew she wasn't ready to do that yet. But she was also remembering his liking for the super-smart restaurants frequented by the

Florentine élite. Etiquette was everything in those places, along with a seriously adhered-to code of dress.

'Somewhere small and casual, then,' she said carefully.

He smiled. 'The prompt was not necessary, *cara.*' It was his turn to chide. 'I was thinking of that little place we used to go to off *Via Delle Belle Donne*—you loved the *panzanella* there, if I recall...'

Its warm, cosy atmosphere was just what Shannon needed. She relaxed again. The food was delicious and the man she shared it with was—perfect.

He sat across a small table with the candlelight flickering on his golden face and fed her small titbits of food with the tips of his long fingers, plied her with a crisp, dry white wine. And he talked, mesmerising her with deep-timbred tones soaked in intimacy and he did it in Italian to force her to concentrate only on him. When she spoke he dipped his eyes to watch her mouth move, kissed it with those eyes to make her lips tremble, then flicked his gaze back to her eyes to make her aware that he knew what was happening to her.

It was the foreplay in a long seduction, she knew, because she'd been caught up in its spell so many times before. He was making love to her with his eyes, with his voice, with every intimate weapon he had in his super-sensual armoury.

'Why?' she asked him suddenly.

'Because I want you,' he answered, not even attempting to misunderstand the question.

Faults and all? she was about to challenge when his fingertips came up to rest against her mouth. 'Don't question me—ask yourself what you want.'

She wanted him, she admitted. She had always wanted him. She wanted tonight to go on for ever and the past to disappear altogether and for the sadness of tomorrow to never come.

So when he kissed her as they left the restaurant she let him, his hands gently crushing her shoulders beneath his leather jacket, the light brush of the bodies a teasing taster for what was to come.

On the way back to the car Luca suddenly left her side with a murmured excuse and disappeared into one of the little shops that sold everything. He came out a few minutes later carrying a box, which he handed to Shannon with a lopsided grin. It was a box of chocolate-coated truffles, more confirmation of what they were going to be doing soon because they always used to indulge in chocolate-coated truffles, feeding them to each other while reclining on the bed, still wearing the bloom on their naked flesh from a long, slow loving.

He was pulling out all of the stops here to recreate their old magic. And she was so busy blushing that she almost missed his other hand slipping something small into his pocket, and even then she just assumed it was some folded paper Euros and dismissed the incident to the back of her head in favour of—other things.

They continued walking towards *Duomo* with anticipation beating a tender pulse of its own. They got into his car as that pulse grew quicker. They drove without speaking, which speeded it all the more. They climbed out of the car and arrived at the basement lift. He reached out to press the call button at the same time that his other hand drew her close.

'You're trembling,' he said.

She tried a laugh that didn't quite work, then his mouth was capturing hers and they were kissing so deeply she was unaware that the lift had arrived until he broke away to manoeuvre them inside its cool metal casing. Then he was propping her up against the wall with his body while he activated security. They rode the lift with his hands cupping her hips, and his lips pressing small kisses all over her face.

She did not push him away. She did not say no to this, so why was she beginning to feel anxious the closer they came to that point at which she was going to move beyond the point of saying no?

The lift doors opened; their bodies separated as they stepped out.

Everything was the same—*everything*. The cream walls, the inlaid floor—Apollo standing to one side of the arch. Electric lights burned, softly activated by a time switch so no one ever arrived here in the dark.

She moved on legs that felt like sponge now, her heart beating oddly in her breast.

Did she want this?

Luca was behind her—close behind her. The lift doors closed and he was turning her round to face him again, capturing her eyes and keeping the past safely merged with the present with the luxurious dark promise burning in his. His jacket was taken from her shoulders and tossed aside on a nearby chair. His hands replaced it, closing over slender shoulders, then stroking down her arms before moving to the tingling base of her spine where he pressed her into arching contact with his body and recaptured her mouth with a deep, deep kiss that sent the question marks flying away.

They moved on to her bedroom, the door closing them into their carefully constructed world where no outside forces were allowed to intrude. She put the box of truffles aside on a chest of drawers, then wound her slender arms around his neck, her head tilting sideways as her mouth searched for his again, lips parted, warm and pulsing with invitation. The breath shuddered from him as he accepted the invitation and he shuddered again when she rolled her tongue around the inner tissues of his mouth. They were joined—already—even without the rest of what was to come. It had always been like this for them.

They kissed like that for ages, immersing themselves in a deep, dark, sensual mist. He stroked her arms, he stroked her body, he slid his hands beneath her hair and slowly slid down the zip to her dress. She sighed at the pleasurable caress of his fingers against the silk-smooth flesh on her back, stretching and arching in perfect accord with his demands as he urged her arms down so he could peel the dress away. The tight cuffs on the sleeves snagged on her hands and he gave a sharp tug to get them free. Then he was collecting up her wrists and kissing them as if to soothe away that small piece of violence—because violence had not been allowed to come into this room with them. It belonged to the past when they'd fallen on each other in a rage of untrammelled lust.

No, she thought, don't remember that, as another moment of indecision feathered her skin.

The dress slithered to the floor, and Luca followed its progress with the dark glow of his eyes while his hands moved on to unclip her bra. Pretty cups of blue lace trailed away from two pale globes with protruding crests of tight rose-pink. He licked one of them and she released a gasp of pleasure, closing her eyes on that unwanted moment of question in favour of this. Her shoulders went back, her head tilting with them so as to lift her breasts up towards his mouth.

Luca laughed; it was a soft and low sound of recognition. She had always been a delightfully receptive lover. He moved his tongue to the other breast and elicited the same response. In the right mood he could make her come just by standing here doing this and nothing else.

But not tonight, he told himself as he sent his hands stroking across skin like satin, gently moulding her slender body then bringing the arching of her hips into contact with the waiting thickness between his. She felt the thrust of his penis and moved against it, instinctive and unreserved when it came to pleasuring the senses.

'Undress me,' he said.

She opened her eyes, blue slow to focus, but smiling a

siren's sensual smile when they did. She reached out to free buttons, smoothing back fabric to reveal the power built into his chest and scraping fingernails through the dark springy hair that covered finely leathered dark golden skin. The shirt fell away and she leant forward to trail wet, warm kisses from one bulging pectoral to the other while her fingers went to unzip his trousers so they could slide inside to explore.

It was a touch like no other. Luca closed his eyes as a wave of desire rolled over him. His breath scored his throat and she whispered something incoherent. When he opened his eyes he saw her tongue running a moist circle around her lips and he knew why it was doing it.

She could hide nothing—never could. Heat roared up from the pit of his very essence and on a growl he picked her up and took her to the bed, bent to throw back the quilt, then laid her on the cool white sheet. She watched him strip off his clothes, still hiding nothing of what she wanted as she followed his movements with her sensual eyes and matched them by stripping away stockings and blue panties, long legs slithering against white linen giving him tantalising glimpses of womanly folds hidden within a burnished copper cloud.

His mouth wanted to swoop and take possession. But not yet, he thought and gave his hand the pleasure of sliding between those restless thighs as he came down beside her, leaving his mouth free to take what it needed from her hungry, hunting mouth.

They kissed, they touched, they rolled together; when he plunged fingers inside her she groaned in shuddering delight. He knew everything about her, where to touch, what to do to launch her into space.

'Need you,' she kept on saying over and over. 'Need you—need you,' until he was dizzy with hearing it, with triumph, with a need of his own that piled on the heat.

Her hands weren't still. He might know Shannon inside and out but she was as well acquainted with him. She knew where to stroke to get his senses roaring, she knew how to torment him and earn herself a flame-hot response, until his blood sang and his breathing became ragged. By the time he let her guide him into her he was already lost to everything but her and this raging pleasure.

She arched her hips in hungry welcome; he made his deep, plunging thrusts without holding anything back. She clung where she could and he rode her like a man chasing after something he should never have lost. The heat of her electrified his senses, her tightness enclosed the length of his shaft. Their mouths were fused, their hearts thundering, their flesh bathed in sweat, limbs gripping or clinging, all parts of them trembling in a hot and gasping journey towards the mercurial finish.

She toppled first, taking him with her, the rippling response of her orgasm fiercely exciting his own. He groaned and kept on groaning with each shuddering stab of his body that released his juices into the path of pulsating muscles that greedily gathered them in.

Eventually it slowed, the tight, speeding rush of the senses steadied, tension eased and he became aware that Shannon was taking his full weight. He slid away from her, then lay on his back with his eyes closed, waiting for the silver-white flood of deep satiation to become a slow ebb.

After a while he found the energy to look at her. She hadn't moved at all. Levering himself up onto a forearm, he looked down to find that her eyes were still closed and she looked quite pale. Had he hurt her? Anxiety shot tension back into his shoulders because he could have done; there had been moments there when he had been lost in a blackness that had roared in his head.

'OK?' he asked huskily and touched his lips to her soft

lips, then gently fingered some damp strands of hair from her cheek.

Her lazy, 'Mmm,' swam through him in a river of relief.

'Then open your eyes and look at me,' he commanded. 'I don't like it when you lie so still.'

Her eyelids fluttered upwards, dusky lashes spiky with mascara—and she smiled. 'You're so wonderful, do you know that?' she told him softly.

In true macho style he agreed with a lazy grin, then touched another kiss to her lips. He had just enjoyed the most amazing experience in his entire life and managed to take his woman along with him. So he felt wonderful.

'Truffles,' she announced suddenly, and was going from satiated stillness into live-wire movement within the single blink of an eye.

Allowing her to wriggle from beneath him, Luca lay on his side and watched through slumber-dark mocking eyes as she climbed off the bed and strode across the room to collect the box of chocolate-coated truffles from where she had placed them on the chest of drawers by the door.

The moment that Shannon picked up the box, something began to nag at her from the back of her mind. She turned round slowly, frowning down at the chocolate-coated truffles while trying to capture whatever that niggling something was.

It was then that it hit like a blinding flashback bursting forth to replay itself. She saw Luca coming out of the shop wearing that smile on his face as he handed her the truffle box. But it was what his other hand was doing that she was focusing on now. She'd thought he'd been sliding some folded Euros into his pocket. She could see it so clearly now that she couldn't believe she had made such a stupid mistake!

He hadn't gone into that shop to buy truffles! Those had

been a mere afterthought to the more serious purchase he'd made.

A packet of condoms. He had bought condoms in preparation for the carefully nurtured love-fest!

'I cannot look at you without wanting to be inside you,' he murmured in a low, dark rasp.

Her chin jerked as she lifted her face to look at him. He was lying in typical, relaxed Luca fashion, on his side with his dark head propped up on a hand and a long, powerful leg casually bent. The naked pose hid nothing. Not the breadth of his chest or the length of his long torso covered with dark hair. Nor did it cover that other cluster of hair that surrounded his sex.

A proud and very potent sex.

She began to shake, with rage or with terror—she wasn't sure which and it was probably a combination of both.

'You bastard,' she spat at him. 'I hate you!'

CHAPTER SIX

'COSA?' Luca's languid dark eyes showed surprise and bewilderment.

'I h-hate you,' Shannon repeated. 'You *knew* you'd done it without the first time and you didn't bother to tell me!'

He sat up, a frown pulling his black brows together across the bridge of his nose. 'What are you talking about?'

'Condoms,' she enlightened. 'Y-you bought some tonight from the shop you got these truffles from. I saw you put them in your trouser pocket.'

'Sì,' he confirmed, not seeing the problem. 'We tempted fate the last time,' he admitted. 'I was not going to take the same chances this time—why are you looking at me like that?'

Because it was getting worse by the second. With a start of screaming alarm, Shannon dropped the box of truffles to make a dive for his trousers where they lay discarded on the floor. Trembling fingers dipped into a pocket and came out with a cellophane wrapped packet.

She didn't even need to speak. Luca saw the packet and caught on at last. *'Idiota,'* he breathed, then had the absolute utter gall to offer her a lazily sheepish grin. 'We never did like those things, did we *cara*? Too much messing around when we were under the influence of much more compelling forces.'

She threw the packet at him. It impacted with a god-like bronze shoulder then dropped with ironic accuracy onto his lap. 'I will never forgive you,' she snapped at him furiously. 'How could you take such risks with me, Luca? How could you!' she cried.

He stared at her for a moment longer, then his own mood altered. 'We both took the risks, *cara*,' he pointed out grimly. 'We fell upon each other without doing much thinking at all, if you recall. It was not a one-way slaking.'

'I wasn't trying to say it was!'

'Then what are you so mad about?' he snapped, rolling off the bed to land on his feet on the other side of it.

She could barely get any words out across the lump of incredulous fury strangling her throat. 'I'm standing here in real danger of already being pregnant and you wonder why I'm mad?' she choked.

'Pregnant? What is this?' he demanded. 'You take the pill,' he stated with supreme confidence, 'and this kind of joke is not funny!'

'You can bet it's not funny,' Shannon breathed hotly. 'Because I am *not* on the pill—why the heck do you think I'm so upset?'

A thick silence clogged up the air for a second. Then, '*Madre di Dio*,' he muttered, 'we have been talking about different risks.'

'What different risks?' she shot at him, bewildered.

'Why are you not on the pill?' he shot back.

'Why did you buy condoms if you believed I was?'

He didn't answer. Instead he grabbed the back of his neck and swung his back to her, leaving Shannon to use up the next few suffocating seconds drawing her own conclusions, which she did with a shuddering gasp of dismay. 'Is what you're *not* saying here,' she framed very slowly, 'that you've been indulging in unsafe sex with other women and *still* didn't think to protect me for my health?'

'I don't believe this conversation.' He turned on her angrily. 'I do not indulge in unsafe sex and I am perfectly healthy!'

'Oh, you're so very positive about that!' she snapped.

'*Sì!*' he declared.

'If that's so and you obviously thought I was taking the pill, then why did you bother to buy the—?'

The answer arrived before she'd even finished asking the question. The sudden taut cast that arrived on his face was like a physical slap of confirmation. The condoms had been bought to protect *him*. He thought *he* was at risk from *her*.

Shannon stopped trembling. It was amazing, she realised, how calming the ice-cold wash of truth could be. She was the bad guy here, the one that took different men to her bed.

And he was the man who had hurt her once too often.

'Get out of my room,' she said, then turned and walked into the bathroom, thrusting the door shut behind her with a foot as she went.

The door didn't even make it into its housing before it was thrust open again by an angry hand. 'I did not mean what you thought I meant,' a still-naked Luca uttered stiffly.

'Yes, you did.' Snatching a bathrobe from the hook behind the door, she wrapped herself in it.

'I denied your charge,' he defined angrily, 'which did not mean I was then throwing the blame onto you!'

No, Shannon thought bitterly, his silence did that for him.

'But we have been apart for two years and no one—man or woman—in their right minds takes unnecessary risks these days!'

'You did—twice!' she flashed.

'And so, *mia cara*, did you,' he returned.

There was no answer to that so she didn't offer one; instead she picked up a towel and tossed it at him. 'Cover yourself,' she said with contempt and went to push past him, but he stayed her with a hand on her arm.

'Stay right where you are,' he commanded darkly. 'We have a problem here and we need to talk about it.'

'I think we've done enough of that.' She tried to tug free.

But he was not going to let her. 'Two years ago you took

the legs from under me,' he threw at her harshly. 'Now here you are doing the same thing to me again!'

'Where do you think my legs are?' she cried. 'You've just issued me with the worst insult a man can pay the woman he's just sank his body into!'

He winced. 'I apologise.'

'It's not enough,' she tugged.

His fingers tightened. 'Then what do you want me to say?'

'Nothing!' She was feeling so chilled it was as if she had ice running in her veins. 'I just want you to leave this room.'

'But I can't do that. You could be carrying my child—'

'Oh—don't *say* that!' She rounded on him, hair flying, face white, tears beginning to blacken her eyes. 'I don't *want* to have your baby!'

He paled. 'You may not be left with the luxury of choice!'

If anything put the lid on the whole wretched mess, then that declaration did. A strangled sob escaped. Luca answered it with a teeth-grinding curse, then let go of her arm and moved away from her, wrapping the towel around the lean, bronzed, tightly moulded buttocks as he went.

Spying the box of truffles lying on the floor, he stooped to pick it up and put it back on the chest of drawers with a thump that said a lot about the feelings rumbling inside him. His hand went back to his neck, grimly grabbing onto the rod of tension that was threatening to snap muscle there.

One part of him was searching for words that would put right the ugliness of what had just happened, but another part—the angry part—was telling him to let it drop because the truth was the truth, even when it was a bitter-tasting truth.

He *had* been thinking of himself with the risk thing. She *did* have a sexual history he could not afford to ignore. How many different 'boyfriends' names had Keira dotted into conversations in her stubborn, stubborn determination to keep Shannon's name alive in his head? Had Keira really believed that it made him feel great to know that Shannon was getting on with her life while his own stagnated?

Keira… He'd allowed himself to forget about Keira and his brother Angelo in this madness. He released a sigh, closing his eyes on a picture of his beautiful but slightly obsessive sister-in-law who used to remind him of a fragile spark of electricity travelling along an endless loop of wire supported by the strong, patient, loving Angelo. That spark had been snuffed out now along with its support, leaving behind a shattered family, an orphaned baby girl and Shannon, who had been knocked about enough by this tragedy without him knocking her about some more.

Dio, he thought. It was not supposed to be like this. Hurting Shannon had not been part of his plan. His sole objective when they'd set out this afternoon had been to remind her how good it used to be between them, not how ugly it could be. He'd wanted her receptive to what they could have again if they both wanted it badly enough—before he'd meant to hit her with his big proposition.

On the bed, after the loving, while sharing a chocolate-coated truffle. His planning had been meticulous. He even had a bottle of champagne and two glasses chilling in the fridge ready to help them celebrate after she'd said yes to his carefully rehearsed speech.

Now all he had was a block of ice standing somewhere behind him hating his guts, which left him wondering heavily what the hell was he supposed to do now to rescue the situation?

Then—*Dio*, he thought again. Where was his head? Nothing had changed here except the mood in which the next part took place and the main thrust of his argument!

Lowering his hand from his neck, he turned to face her. She was still standing in the bathroom doorway looking about as receptive to reason as a cat would be to the mouse it held in its teeth.

Was he a mouse? The hell that he was, he thought grimly and braced himself in readiness for what he was going to say next. 'Marry me,' he announced, reducing his well rehearsed and reasoned speech to the basic bottom line of it. 'Then all of this stops being a problem.'

A cold stone block of silence followed. Shannon continued to stare at him through those sapphire eyes and he received a very, very erotic sensation across his neck that made him think of cats and mice and—teeth.

Then she moved, and the erotic sensation slithered down his body to pool around his sex. 'Well, it must have hurt you to say that,' she drawled deridingly.

'No,' he denied.

Shannon felt her mouth flick out a cold little smile in response. Did he think she hadn't noticed the way he'd had to brace himself before making that outrageous suggestion?

And outrageous it was after what they'd just exchanged. He still hated and resented her beneath all of that throbbing desire she could see pounding at his magnificent chest. She was sure of it now—how could she not be?

'I am not having your baby.' She stated it firmly, grabbing the crux of this proposal and crushing the life out of it before it became a terrifying monster in her head. 'And even if I was unfortunate enough to be pregnant, I only have to think about Keira to gauge my chances of carrying a baby full term.'

'Don't say that.' He frowned. 'You are not your sister. You—'

'So for us to consider marriage on the slimmest chance of my being pregnant is really stupid,' she interrupted him. 'But, even if I *am* pregnant and *did* manage to carry the baby full term, I would *not* marry a man who thinks that not only am I promiscuous but I'm irresponsible with it!'

'I don't think you are promiscuous!' he denied. 'And we are not getting back into that.'

As far as Shannon was concerned they'd never left it! 'Can't trust me to stay faithful, then!'

He thrust out his chin. 'I can trust,' he insisted.

Her own chin went up, blue eyes defying the lying swine to prove that statement. 'Who was I planning to be with the night you came to my London flat?' she challenged.

His frown dragged the two black bars of his eyebrows together. 'How should I know?'

'You heard me make two telephone calls—both of which were to men—and drew some pretty quick assumptions that both of them were my lovers! That makes me pretty sluttish and untrustworthy wife material, don't you think? Add those two lovers to my irresponsible behaviour regarding sex and either one of them could be the father of this fictitious child!'

He dismissed that line of argument with an impatient flick of one long-fingered hand. 'One of those calls was to a woman.'

Surprise widened her eyes. 'Who told you that?'

'Joshua Soames,' he replied. 'He called here the other day to talk to you while you were at the hospital. I asked the question, he set the record straight.'

He'd actually pumped her business partner for information about Alex? 'And you call that trusting me?'

The frown darkened. 'Stop this,' he grated. 'Do you think I am an idiot? If you are not on the pill then you are not in a relationship. And don't start going on about slutting,' he dismissed with another flick of that hand when she opened her mouth to answer him. 'This is too serious an issue to be bouncing insults off each other. If you are pregnant it will be because I made you so, in which case I want to be there for you. If you have to go through what Keira went through, then I want to be there to support you as Angelo supported Keira. So I am offering you a serious commitment here.' He began walking towards her, closing a gap Shannon did not want closed. 'I am offering marriage—now—before the timing of conception can become an issue. I am offering it without any prejudice from the past getting in the way. And I would appreciate an honest and unprejudiced answer from you instead of razor sarcasm.'

Shannon stood through it all, watching his face and his expressive hands in fascination while listening to the slick dynamics of his clever brain as he put together his offer outlining all the positives for marriage and ignoring the negatives such as—no love, no respect, no emotional commitment, no mention of his family's horrified response.

She felt like a business he was trying to take over. He was being very cool and practical and even a little arrogant, though the arrogance was rather an attractive feature of his sales pitch. His ulterior motive? For the moment she couldn't think of one, she was too engrossed in the seductive power this man possessed when he turned himself into a trouble-shooter. She'd always liked it, been an absolute sucker for it once upon a time. Get him in professional mode discussing the rudiments of corporate management and she would be stripping him naked as he talked.

She'd seen him work this kind of magic on a room full of hard headed women while giving a talk at a businesswomen's convention. By the time he'd stepped off the podium to rapturous applause there had not been a woman in the place who had not been fantasising about him. She had been the lucky one to get him alone, though, and tap into the fantasy.

She could feel the same charismatic pull now trying to draw her towards him like a magnet. The voice was seductive, the beautiful accent was seductive, the expressive way he used his hands made you visualise them moving over your skin. The serious mouth that pretended he did not know it was happening was seductive; the serious eyes that waited politely for her to offer her response were seducing her into uttering the response he wanted to hear.

He was lethal, she acknowledged. But she'd also come up with the answer to his ulterior motive.

Sex.

He might be able to keep the mask of his face under control but he was not having the same luck with the rest of his body. He'd said at much before as he lay on the bed watching her as she went to get the box of truffles. 'I cannot look at you without wanting to be inside you,' he'd confessed. What they could do for each other was still jumping all over his senses with a desire to do it all again and again.

He was hooked, on the slut who always did have the instinctive sensual expertise to turn him inside out. So—why not marry her? was his very male answer to a nagging problem. If her betrayal with another man had not got in the way two years ago, he would have committed himself to her body and soul then and without a single regret for his lost single status. He was still prepared to do that because, despite all that had happened, the sex was still mindlessly good. And the irresistible little sweetener to his outrageous proposal was that he could have it all without all the old emotional stuff getting in the way.

She called it thinking on his feet, seeing a chance to have his cake and eat it at the same time. Somewhere in the last hour she had been elevated to his idea of the perfect woman. A woman, in other words, who would be absolutely great to have as a permanent fixture in his bed but would not expect or get anything else from him once they were out of that bed.

The bastard, she thought. He hadn't bothered to mention his darling family or the fact that they had all just lived through the worst seven days of all of their lives and still had the worst day to come. This was a window of opportunity and he was not going to let the chance pass by.

She felt cold—iced over by his calculation, the speed with which he could assess and decide. He had done it to her before—two years ago in this very apartment when he'd walked in on a frankly suspicious scene, assessed and come to a decision with the blinding speed of light. That was the moment that she'd become a slut in his eyes and nothing she said afterwards could change that belief.

She shivered, she felt so cold. Inside—outside—and found herself fighting a battle with her tongue that wanted her to blurt out the truth. What would he do if she brought it all out into the open again? she wondered. Would he respond as he had done the last time by accusing her of daring to soil her sister with her own sins?

And what had Keira done? she then recalled painfully. Her sister had begged her to say nothing. Begged her to understand why she could never confess the truth to Luca, not even for Shannon's sake. 'He will tell Angelo. How could he not? If it was the other way round I would have to tell you or I could not live with myself!'

Those words were emblazoned on her heart for ever now. Because despite everything Keira had said she *had* told Luca, she had tried to save herself at the expense of Keira's marriage to Angelo.

But Luca had refused to believe.

Keira had been everyone's vision of the perfect woman, therefore Shannon had to be the sinner.

His opinion was not about to change because he'd discovered he could not keep his hands off her. He was still going to go on resenting her presence in his life and never trusting her alone with any man and probably using the sex as a darn great way of exacting punishment for betraying him.

So, did she say—Believe me about Keira and I might consider your proposition, or did she say—?

'My answer is no,' she announced, then turned and walked back into the bathroom, having the sense to shoot home the bolt this time before she sank down onto the toilet seat to bury her face in her trembling hands and silently cried her eyes out.

Because she knew that despite the long, hard lecture she had been a tongue tip away from tarnishing her poor sister's image in his eyes for ever by insisting he listen to the truth. She even had proof to back her story up, though not here, but back in London.

Luca stood with the sound of that bolt sliding home ringing in his ears and was damned hellish angry for opening himself up to that cold little no.

Who did she think she was, turning down his frankly very generous offer? She was lucky to be getting one. Did she think he wanted to attach himself to a natural-born siren with eyes constantly on the lookout for the next man?

But she was carrying his child. In his mind it was already a statement of fact—it had to be or his arguments crumbled to dust at his feet. If the witch believed he was going to allow her to walk away carrying that child with her, then she was in for a very big shock.

Turning on his heel, he walked out of her room and down the hall into his own room. Once safely shut away in there he went to take a shower—while planning his next line of attack.

There was a moment once his anger had cooled and he began to think like a rational man again that he questioned what the hell it was he was trying to do to himself by getting involved with her again.

Trust? He could never trust her out of his sight! Shannon had been right when she had faced him with that.

Did he really want a future of forever wondering who she was with when she wasn't with him?

No, he damn well did not.

Of course he could not trust her. Just as he could not dare to trust his own judgement where she was concerned, because if anyone had suggested to him that she was playing around behind his back two years ago he would have laughed in their faces—before knocking them flat.

The old dark feelings returned with a vengeance. Pushing his head beneath the shower spray, he rinsed off shampoo and saw images of that afternoon when he had come home unexpectedly to find Shannon standing in the doorway to the bedroom trying to block him from seeing the truth.

And what a truth. 'What are you doing back?' She could not have appeared more horrified to see him.

'I could ask you the same question. You were supposed to be in London until tomorrow.'

'I came back early.' She tried pulling the bedroom door shut behind her.

'So did I,' he answered absently. 'I needed some papers from my safe…' Instinct made him step around her and push the door open again.

'Damn,' he muttered as soap got in his eye. Switching off the shower, he reached for a towel and tried not to let his mind take him into that room as he wiped the stinging soap away.

The room was a mess. The bedding pulled back and lying half on the floor. He picked up the scent of male cologne. Not his cologne, not his red silk boxer shorts that he pulled quite calmly from the tangle of white sheeting. He never wore silk underwear; he never wore red. He preferred cotton, black, white, grey—any damn colour but red.

'Who do these belong to?' He saw himself swing round in time to catch her sliding something into a bedside drawer.

'I came back to f-find it like this. I don't know wh-what—'

His hand reached out to open the drawer Shannon had pushed shut. He saw her stiffen then start to tremble, then lower her eyes when he drew out the packet of condoms.

Condoms, bloody condoms, he thought viciously. The blight of his bloody life!

One was missing—not that it mattered that one was missing; the fact that they were there at all was enough to turn his blood to bile. They did not use condoms. And that scent—that damned strong male scent had clung to his nostrils while he'd stood there trying to deal with what it was he was being forced to face.

'I can explain…' She'd sounded deep-voiced and husky, like someone suffering from an intolerable amount of anxiety and stress.

Without saying a word he put the packet back in the drawer and closed it, then turned to look at her. 'Before you jump to your rotten conclusions—it wasn't me, Luca, it wasn't me!'

'Who, then?' he challenged.

Her face was white, her eyes black pools of utter torment; tears trailed down her cheeks and worked at her throat. 'Keira,' she whispered.

Keira. Of all the lying excuses she could have come up with, she had to choose to place the blame on the one person who would never betray her man—never. Her willingness to do that to her own sister broke his calm. What followed had been another nightmare that had lived inside him ever since.

A telephone began ringing somewhere, bringing him out of the blackness of that second nightmare to discover that he was standing in the bathroom staring at the ceramic tiles covering the floor where water was dripping from his body to form a pool around his brown feet. He lifted his head and caught sight of his face in the mirror. It was not him. It was like looking at a stranger. A man with no colour and no warmth.

Only Shannon could do this to him.

And he had offered her marriage again?

Pulling on a bathrobe, he made himself walk on legs that felt oddly stiff, as if he had just run a marathon. Maybe he had done—run a marathon through agony, lies and deceit.

He had left his jacket on the chair by the lift. His mobile phone was in one of its pockets and he strode through the apartment to collect it. The call was from Marco, his assistant. He frowned at the lateness of the hour and felt a hard snap of irritation because if Marco was still in the office then he was probably being snowed under trying to keep up in his absence.

He was bringing the call to an end when Shannon appeared in the archway. She was wearing the skimpy blue pyjamas beneath a thin blue cotton wrap, which hung open down her front. Her face was scrubbed and shiny, her hair piled up on top of her head leaving her slender neck exposed. Her eyes were like two dark bruises set on a background of porcelain white and her mouth looked tiny, pinched and—pink.

Hunger roared to life inside him followed by a self-contempt that wrapped itself like a steel band around his chest. He turned his back on her to listen in grim silence to whatever it was Marco was asking him. The poor devil sounded harassed and bone weary. Luca knew both feelings. Shannon still hovered in the archway; he wondered what she wanted.

'Just leave it for tonight, Marco,' he commanded quietly. 'The business is not going to go down the tubes if you go home and get some sleep.'

He ended the call and dropped the phone onto his jacket,

then had to flex his shoulders before he could bring himself to turn and face Shannon again.

She blinked at the toughness hardening his features. 'I'm sorry to intrude,' she apologised stiffly. 'But we left my shopping in the car and I need to hang up my suit…'

He sighed at the stupid oversight and the pendulum swing of his emotions took yet another violent swerve. What kind of selfish bastard was he to be adding to her stress at a time like this?

Misreading the reason for his sigh, she walked towards him with her hand outstretched. 'If you let me have your car keys I'll go and collect the bags myself.'

Let her loose in a basement car park at this time of the night dressed like this? 'Not while I still breathe,' he hissed, making her frown because she didn't understand.

And he was not going to enlighten her.

'I'll go,' was all he said, and turned to get his wallet and car keys from where he'd placed them on the table by the lift.

She was waiting at her bedroom door when he came back with her shopping bags.

'Thank you.' She took them from him.

'Prego,' he replied.

She took a step back, and closed the door in his face.

A sudden blistering urge to push the damn door open again and have this out almost had him doing just that. Then common sense arrived and along with it a burst of frustration, which had him aiming a clenched fist that didn't quite land on the oak panelling.

Then he went back to his own room to fester in silence.

While Shannon threw herself down on the bed to cry her eyes out again.

She hated him but she loved him and that was her toughest problem—she loved, loved—*loved* the brute!

* * *

The next day was a day Shannon hoped she would never have to endure again. From the moment she donned the black outfit the full weight of what she was about to face took her deep, deep inside herself.

She met Luca in the foyer. A fleeting glance at him standing there in his sombre black suit, white shirt and black tie, his lean face drawn into a pale grey mask of steely composure, and she knew he was feeling the same way she did. He studied her briefly, taking in her own waxen composure before he enquired expressionlessly if she was ready to leave.

Fredo drove them in a black limousine that made no attempt to disguise what it was. Even the day had decided to wear a grey cloud cast as if it knew that this was not a day to fill with warm sunlight.

They didn't talk; both had their faces half turned to the car's side windows, preferring to remain sunk into their own bleak thoughts.

They barely touched unless Luca was taking her arm to politely help her in or out of the car.

They arrived at his mother's house to find that the whole vast and scattered Salvatore family had congregated. Everyone was subdued, grave, but kind and sympathetic towards Shannon, which was nice of them given their knowledge of her past relationship with Luca—not that anyone but the closest family members knew what had happened, only that they'd parted under bitter circumstances. But still, Shannon appreciated their willingness to put all of that aside for today at least—though some could not help throwing curious glances at herself and Luca, who was never more than a step away from her side, though they did not acknowledge each other's presence.

From the moment they stepped out of the house everything took on a bleak, dreamlike quality that led them frame by agonising frame through the ensuing hours. Mrs

Salvatore was bereft. Each time she broke down the whole sombre gathering felt its rippling effect. And it was heart-rending to watch her cling to her surviving son as if she was afraid to let go in case he was lost to her too.

Renata and Sophia clung to their husbands, Tazio and Carlo. One sister was older than her surviving brother, the other slotting in between Luca and Angelo. Both were stunningly beautiful, as were all the Salvatores, and their two men had been picked to complement their outstanding looks and great name.

Shannon clung to no one, though she knew that Luca somehow always managed to keep himself within arm's reach of her just in case she broke down, but she didn't; she just kept her head lowered and did her grieving silently beneath her black lace veil.

She almost cracked at her first sighting of the two flower-decked coffins. And again later when she stepped into the church and was shocked by how many more people there were packed into it. Friends and colleagues, she presumed, most of whom were strangers to her but not to Angelo and Keira. In her heart all these people represented life surrounding the tragic couple as they made their journey to their final resting place.

She didn't shed tears throughout the service. She didn't do anything other than go where she was instructed to go, sit, stand, kneel, wait—follow. The waxen mask of her composure took its worst beating during the graveside ceremony. Mrs Salvatore almost collapsed and Luca had to support her in both his arms. Sophia wept, Renata wept, the whole flower-bedecked site seemed to rock beneath the rolling weight of everyone's grief.

Afterwards they made the journey to the Salvatore family villa set high above Florence on the outskirts of Fiesole. It was a beautiful place steeped in the fabulous trappings of wealth collected over centuries and surrounded by the most exquisite gardens big enough to lose yourself in. It was a place used by all factions of the Salvatore family for throwing extravagant parties. Today it became a place shrouded in sorrow, where the whole congregation gathered to pay their respects to the family.

Mrs Salvatore was led away to her private apartments so she could have a few minutes to compose herself. Luca, his two sisters and their husbands took up the role of hosts as the many formal reception rooms began to fill with black-clad sombre people and sober-dressed serving staff that mingled amongst them carrying white-linen-covered silver trays holding a choice of refreshment.

And Shannon had never felt so lost and alone in her entire life as she did as she wandered aimlessly from room to room, smiling politely at those who offered her their sympathy and murmuring all the right phrases in response, but she felt strange inside, oddly out of place as if she did not belong here and she knew why she felt that way.

She had just buried her sister, yet she felt as if her right to grieve had been hijacked by this great, heaving wave of Salvatore grief. It was silly, selfish and unfair of her to think this way, but telling herself that did not remove the feeling. Everyone spoke in Italian and she wanted to speak English. She wanted to remember her sister in their own language and scream at the top of her voice— Let me have my sister back!

Someone caught her arm as she was stepping out of one room into another and she was hustled into a quiet alcove set into the side of the grand staircase. Luca loomed over her like a dark shadow.

'The British stiff upper lip is still in use, I see,' he drawled sardonically.

CHAPTER SEVEN

IF HE only knew what was going on inside her head, Shannon thought. 'I didn't see you showing signs of letting your composure crack,' she countered distantly.

'It is cracked inside—bleeding, in fact.' Luca surprised her with the gruff admission. 'Here, drink some of this,' he said and put a glass in her hand.

'What is it?' she asked suspiciously.

'Brandy. It might help warm you up. You look in danger of turning into an ice sculpture.'

She drank some of the brandy and was annoyed with herself afterwards because it went straight to her eyes.

'Don't,' Luca husked.

'You started it,' she blamed, stretching her eyes wide to stop the tears, and lifted a set of fingers to press them against her trembling mouth.

His sigh arrived with the gentle touch of a long finger as it brushed a stray lock of hair from her cheek. It was contact enough to make her want to throw her arms around his neck and sob her heart out.

Someone appeared on the periphery of their vision. It was Renata; she took one look at the intimacy of their little one-to-one and tensed. Luca's older sister was one the nicest people anyone would wish to meet, but she struggled to look at Shannon without showing her disapproval.

'Mama has come down and is asking for you, Luca,' she informed her brother stiffly.

'I'll be there in a minute,' he said without taking his eyes from Shannon.

'Mama said—'

'A minute, Renata,' he interrupted incisively.

There was a pause that set the fine hairs on Shannon's body tingling and kept her eyes firmly fixed on the black silk knot of Luca's tie, then Renata spun away leaving an uncomfortable silence behind her.

'That wasn't very nice,' she chided.

'I don't feel like being nice,' he clipped in reply. 'For the whole of this terrible day you have looked like a lonely piece of fragile porcelain someone put down and forgot to pick up again. I want to pick you up and never put you down.'

It was Shannon's turn to murmur an uneven, 'Don't.' He had no right to be saying things like that to her—especially not after the way he'd used her last night.

'We need to talk. Last night was a mess,' he said abruptly, hooking right into her thoughts again. 'It should not have ended the way that it did.'

'I don't want to discuss it.' She made a move to follow in Renata's footsteps.

Luca blocked her exit from the alcove with a broad shoulder that effectively held her captive. 'We have to talk about it,' he insisted. 'There are things I should have said last night that got lost in the war. But they are about to come up and hit us both in the face so I need you to listen.'

'Listen to what—more insults?'

'No,' he denied on a rasp of impatience. 'The marriage thing,' he explained. 'You said no to marrying me for our child's sake but—'

'There is no child!' she inserted sharply.

'Luca…' It was the softer voice of Sophia that interrupted this time, sounding very cautious. 'I am sorry to disturb you but Signor Lorenzo has arrived. He wants to…'

A string of near-silent curses left Luca's lips while Shannon closed her eyes and prayed to God that Sophia hadn't heard what she'd said. 'I'm coming,' he bit out in grinding impatience.

Sophia wasn't up to pushing her point as her older sister had done, because she walked away without saying another word, leaving Shannon trapped in the alcove by a man who was literally pulsing with frustration and a burn in his eyes that made her think of—

Stop it, she thought painfully. Don't *do* this to me here! She dragged in a tense breath. 'Go to your mother, or Mr—whoever,' she said tautly.

But Luca was not going anywhere. 'Just listen,' he instructed, 'because I do not have time for this but I know it must be said!' He took a deep breath, impatience fighting with something Shannon couldn't quite put a name to but it set her trembling as he caught her eyes again and began feeding words to her in a quick, sharp rasp. 'I want you to think about Rose. I want you to put your own feelings aside, and my feelings, for that matter, and think about her and what is best for her.'

'Rose will come home with me. I mean to—'

'No!' he shot at her forcefully. His hands came up to grip her shoulders, the sudden angry shift of his body almost knocking the glass of brandy out of her hand. 'I knew you were planning something like this,' he bit out like a curse, 'but it cannot be like that.'

'Why not?'

'Because—'

'Luca...' There was no dismissing the owner of this particular voice. It belonged to Mrs Salvatore herself. Shannon almost sagged with relief when he let go of her shoulders on a sigh of surrender and turned to his mother.

'Father Michael has to leave now but he says you wanted a word with him before he— Oh, Shannon,' Mrs Salvatore cut off to acknowledge. 'I did not see you standing there.'

Which was a blatant untruth because if this wasn't part

of a conspiracy to stop whatever it was the family believed they were doing in this alcove, then Shannon would eat her hat.

Then she smashed that bit of untimely sarcasm when she saw the devastation written in the older woman's face. Luca's mother had every right to want her remaining son all to herself just now, she thought guiltily, and managed to squeeze past Luca to offer his mother a smile.

'Luca brought me a drink,' she explained.

'So thoughtful of you, Luca,' Mrs Salvatore nodded in approval. 'It seems to have done the trick, Shannon, and put some of the colour back into your cheeks. You needed it, poor dear,' she added on a husky quaver. 'Today has been such an ordeal for all of us.'

'Yes, such an ordeal,' Shannon endorsed as the full power of it came clattering back down upon her head. To her surprise, Mrs Salvatore reached out to put her arms around her and brushed a kiss on both of her cheeks. 'I will miss Keira so much,' she confided thickly—and she said it in English.

It was almost Shannon's undoing. She had to swallow the tears and was able only to nod and return the two kisses because she knew she couldn't speak. Luca's mother seemed to understand that because she patted her gently before releasing her, then turned her attention to her son.

'I don't understand why you need to speak with Father Michael but I don't think you should keep him waiting.'

'No,' her son agreed.

Shannon took this as her cue to make good her escape, 'Excuse me,' she murmured, and was about to melt quietly away when Luca stopped her with the touch of long fingers to her arm. 'OK?' he asked huskily.

She kept her eyes lowered, swallowed and nodded, but he didn't appear impressed. She could feel his irritation, his frustrated desire to finish what he had begun. But he couldn't and he knew that he couldn't. 'Think about what I said,' he clipped out eventually.

Not if I can stop myself, Shannon thought bleakly, but nodded because his mother was listening. Then she slipped her arm free of his fingers and walked away, aware of his eyes following her—aware that his mother's eyes were doing the same.

She looked so damn fragile he knew she was going to have to break soon, Luca was thinking grimly.

'I hope you know what you're doing,' his mother said.

He looked down into the pale, anxious face of this woman he loved without question and wished he could love Shannon that way again. 'I know exactly what I'm doing,' he assured her soberly.

'Still…' his mother heaved in a breath of air '...it is best not to make hasty decisions while you are feeling so vulnerable.'

The comment amused him enough to have him tilt a mocking eyebrow. 'I wish I knew what you were talking about,'

'You and Shannon,' he was informed. 'It only takes a pair of eyes to know that you two are sleeping together.'

'Madre!' he admonished.

'Why else would you insist that she stay at your apartment?' She shrugged off the censure. 'Why else would Shannon refuse my invitation to stay with me? The sparks fly between you like electricity and it took three—*three*—people to prize you out of this alcove.'

'Maybe that was because we did not want to be *prized* out,' Luca suggested dryly.

His mother was not impressed. 'It is a known fact that life clings to life in times of tragedy,' she persisted stubbornly. 'I can understand it—even sympathise with it. I cannot imagine another situation in which the two of you could be thrown together again so powerfully. But you now have Father Michael waiting to talk to you and Angelo's lawyer awaiting his turn. I am concerned about what it is you are planning to do.'

There was a lot he could say in reply to this, but Luca's attention was already fixed elsewhere. Throughout his mother's very sensible lecture his eyes had followed the glowing crown of Shannon's head as she moved amongst the darker heads clustered at the other end of the hall. He'd watched her pause, listen, accept embraces of sympathy, watched her pretend to sip at the glass of brandy she still held in her hand. She seemed fine, composed, coping admirably—yet a niggling sensation was clawing at his instincts.

'Luca, please listen to me,' his mother urged anxiously. 'I don't want to see the two of you hurt each other again!'

His eyelashes gave a reluctant flicker as he made himself look away from Shannon and into his mother's worried face. Lifting his hands to cover his mother's fingers where they rested against his chest, he drew them to his lips to kiss them gently, then firmly lowered them to her sides. 'I love you,' he told her gently. 'It breaks my heart that you let yourself worry about me. But we are going to have to finish this later, *mi amore*...'

Because something more urgent was tugging at him. And to lift his gaze back to the spot where he had last seen Shannon only to discover he couldn't see that distinctive flame head of hers anywhere turned that tug into a roar that had him striding away, passing by the tall, slender figure of Father Michael and the more rotund Emilio Lorenzo without even seeing them.

Where did she go—?

Shannon had opened the door and slipped quietly inside the Salvatore library with its beautiful pale wood-panelled walls and light blue furnishings, and ornately corniced bookcases filled with rows of priceless books. It was quiet in here, and so free of other people that her shoulders dipped in relief. Luca had hustled her into thinking when she did not want to think. Now she had an ache building behind her eyes that was promising to develop into a blinding headache if she didn't snatch a few minutes to herself.

At first she walked across to the window to stare out at the gardens laid out with classical Italian formality and awash with the yellow and purple heads of the season's first spring flowers. There was a moment when she was tempted to open one of the French doors and step out onto the terrace to breathe in some fresh air. But the greyness of the day warned her it was cold out there, and instead she turned to face the room again and was drawn towards the huge white marble fireplace where a burning log fire sent out flickering fingers of inviting warmth.

She was about to sit down in one of the winged chairs flanking the fire when she saw the row of silver framed pictures standing on the mantel top. Her heart gave a pained little flutter as she put down her glass on a small table, then went to study each picture in turn.

They were all there in their wedding finery and standing beneath the same stone archway to the same church they had visited today. Renata with Tazio, Sophia with Carlo—even Mrs Salvatore stood with her handsome husband whom Shannon had never been fortunate enough to meet, but she still knew that if he'd walked by her in the street she would have known who he was because Luca looked so much like him.

And then there was the picture of Angelo and Keira. Reaching up with fingers that weren't quite steady, she gently floated them over the faces of these two happy people she would never see smile like this again. It came then, breaking free on an anguished sob followed by another and another that sent her sinking to her knees where she knelt, hugging herself as she rocked to and fro, pouring out everything she had been so staunchly holding in.

The door flew open and a cluster of people came to a stunned halt in its opening. She didn't know, had no idea that Luca had been causing quite a scene out there because he couldn't locate her. She didn't know that he'd found her until he was dropping to his knees in front of her and was uttering something thick and uneven as he gathered her up against him.

'I can't bear it, I can't bear it,' she could hear herself sobbing as he lowered his dark head over hers, and she could feel the tremors shaking him.

Someone else uttered a broken sob and a different hand arrived at the base of her spine. It was Luca's mother's hand. Despite her concerns Mrs Salvatore was no match for the depth of Shannon's broken-hearted grief. Tears thickened her voice as she offered words of comfort. Over by the door several others struggled to keep their tears in check.

But it was Luca who held her, Luca's composure she could feel tearing apart at its seams.

'*Idiota,*' he muttered as she buried her face in his throat and washed him with the deep, gulping agony of her tears. 'I take my eyes off you for two short seconds and you disappear to do this! Why are you so stubborn?' he demanded unevenly. 'Why do you insist on believing you can carry all of this grief without help from me? Don't I know better? Don't you always fall apart eventually? When we are married I am going to shackle you to my side, then I will not need to—'

'I am not marrying you,' Shannon sobbed into his throat as a chorus of shocked gasps ran around the room. She didn't hear them.

Luca ignored them, his fingers dislodging the clip holding up her hair so the thick, flaming mass uncoiled over his fingers as he pressed her closer. 'Yes you are,' he gritted. 'It is your fate—*my* fate.'

'What are you are saying?' It was Renata who spoke so scandalously.

'Nothing you would not have heard by the end of today,' he supplied while Shannon sobbed all the harder, and he wondered how long he had left before he joined her in all of this agony.

'Then you are a fool!'

'Sì,' he acknowledged. 'Tazio, have Fredo bring the car to the door, if you please,' he requested. 'I am taking Shannon home.'

He climbed abruptly to his feet with Shannon still clamped to the front of him. 'Can you stand or do I carry you?' he asked her.

'I am not going to marry you.' Shannon found strength from Renata's dismay to lift her tear-washed face and burn the words up at him. 'Look at those pictures, Luca—*look*!' she insisted with a wave towards the mantel top. 'They're all happy to be marrying each other. Are we happy? Are *they* happy that you're even thinking of marriage to me?'

Luca did not look at the row of pictures on the mantel top or the real versions of those people who were clustered around the door. He looked at Shannon; he looked *into* Shannon. 'Angelo and Keira will be happy for us,' he stated. 'Their daughter will be happy for us when we adopt her into our new family. And you're—'

Shannon's heart leapt to her throat, 'Don't you dare say it!' she choked out. 'I'm not—'

'Already pregnant with our own precious child?'

The next mass gasp was followed by a comprehensive silence. Mrs Salvatore's hand still lay against Shannon's back, but it was removed jerkily.

'How could you?' Shannon whispered.

'It was surprisingly easy,' Luca mocked her with a look.

'Are you now going to make Renata's wishes come true and make a fool of me again?'

Well, are you? Shannon was forced to ask herself. She looked into the wry, slightly rueful face of this man she had loved for so long she couldn't remember when she began loving him, and thought— No, I won't do it again.

Her tears cleared away, her shaky composure slipped quietly back into place. Moistening her trembling lips, she turned in the circle of his arms and faced this family she had once felt such a welcome part of but now—

'Luca and I are getting married,' she announced in a voice that refused not to shake. 'I'm sorry if you don't like it but its wh-what we both w-want.'

'So we plan to do it next week in a quiet ceremony in respect of our recent loss,' Luca took over. 'You are welcome to attend but it is not a duty I expect you to take up if you cannot bring yourselves to wish us well in this.'

No one spoke—no one. There wasn't a single good luck, God damn you or even a dismissive go to hell, you pair of fools. It was a suffocating, suffocating blanket of perfect silence until—

'Well, bravo,' a smooth male voice commended, and Father Michael detached himself from the small group.

He began walking towards them, a tall, slender man with silver hair and a look of a Salvatore etched in his lean face. He paused to touch slender white sympathetic fingers to Mrs Salvatore's shocked cheek, then continued on until he came to a stop in front of them.

'I now understand your desire to arrange this hasty wedding service, Luca.' He smiled as he reached out to shake his hand. 'This should have happened two years ago, of course, but next week is good. I for one am very happy for you both.'

There were so many hidden messages in what he'd said that it caused a wave of discomfort to shift through their audience. Shannon couldn't cope. She had taken enough. Fresh tears were throbbing in her throat and she knew she was in danger of falling apart again.

She certainly didn't need the priest to swing the attention to her. But that was exactly what he did. 'Welcome to the Salvatore family, Shannon,' he sanctioned, bringing his hands to rest on her shoulders. 'Having come to know your sister well over the years, I know how hard she prayed for this to happen.' He bent to place kisses on both of her cheeks. 'She can be at peace now, *cara*,' he murmured for her ears only. 'For her sake try to be at peace with it yourself.'

It was then that she knew that Father Michael knew everything. Keira must have confessed all to the priest. Her shoulders shook as the tears threatened to burst forth again and she broke free of Luca's arms to sink into one of the winged chairs with different hurts, different emotions, all clamouring to take a bite out of her.

Father Michael moved back across the room, gathering Luca's mother beneath his arm as he went and herding the rest of his subdued flock before him through the door. 'Take the poor child home, Luca. I will stay and deal with the other business you have pending here,' were the final complacent words spoken in the Salvatore library for long seconds after the door closed.

'I can't believe you did that.' Shannon broke into the silence.

'I am having great difficulty believing that you backed me up,' was Luca's drawling reply. 'Here…' The glass of brandy was retrieved from the reading table and slotted between her fingers. 'Drink,' he commanded.

Drink, she repeated and spent a few seconds toying with the idea of tossing the drink in his face. Then Luca asked grimly, 'What did Father Michael say to you that almost had you shattering again?'

And she took a sip at the brandy because she suddenly needed it. 'Nothing,' she mumbled. 'What was the *other* business he mentioned as he left?'

'Last will and testaments,' he supplied. 'Emilio Lorenzo is Angelo's lawyer. He is here to read Angelo and Keira's joint will. But there is one specific section, which deals with the unlikely event of their dying at the same time. It is that part which concerns you and me.'

'What do you mean?' She looked up at him with the question. He was standing with an arm resting against the mantel top, his expression grim as he stared into the leaping log flames.

'If you will accept a loose translation from memory, it says that in the event of both parties dying together their joint estates will be placed into trust for any surviving children they might have. The trust to be administered by you and me.' He shifted his gaze to her face to watch as she absorbed this surprising news. 'We are also given joint guardianship of any children they may have,' he added. 'So, you see, even if you want to adopt Rose for yourself, you cannot without my agreement, just as I cannot adopt her without yours.'

And there was the crux of this marriage business, Shannon realised. Forget everything else. Luca had known about the will all along. He must have felt the noose close around his neck the moment he'd read it because, being who he was, not only was he not going to allow his brother's child to be brought up by anyone but himself, but he was not going to let Shannon have power of say over what had to amount to a large chunk of Salvatore stock without him having power of say over her. Good grief, she could almost see the cogs spinning inside his head at the prospect. If he didn't marry her then she was at liberty to marry someone else—a man, moreover, whom she might allow to dabble his fingers in Salvatore business.

She laughed; it was all suddenly so clear. 'You've had our marriage planned from the moment Keira died, haven't you?' she murmured.

'Yes.' He didn't even bother to lie.

'And the carefully constructed trip down memory lane yesterday, culminating in the big seduction scene, was the precursor to a marriage proposal.'

'I did intend to explain about the will first,' he declared in his own defence.

While sharing chocolate-coated truffles in their bed of passion. 'Shame all of that other stuff about condoms got in your way,' she said.

'We fight like wild cats, *cara*, we always have done,' he reminded her softly. 'Neither of us is inclined to give way.'

Resting her head against the corner of the chair, she looked at him standing there with the firelight playing dynamic tricks with his smoothly handsome face—and wondered why she wasn't angry with him.

Because she'd given up, she realised. He had claimed that neither of them gave way in a fight, but she knew she had given way by backing this marriage thing.

Why? Because she loved the ruthless devil. Because she was being handed an opportunity here that would never come her way again. Father Michael had been right when he'd said it was time for her to be at peace with herself. If being at peace meant letting herself to love Luca, without the old resentments tagging onto it, then she could do that now. The fact that Luca could not allow himself the same peace was not his fault, but the fault of circumstances even she could accept had been pretty damning at the time. But he had loved her once, and if that look in his eyes wasn't telling her he was fighting hard not to love her again then she didn't know him at all.

He was hers. Everything he did and said demonstrated that he was hers. Even this last bit of manipulation had been an act of possession meant to cloak his true feelings or he would not have gone for the all-out seduction last night, but chosen the cool-headed business proposition he'd been forced to put into action only when the seduction had failed.

'When you smile like that the hairs on the back of my neck start to tingle,' he murmured darkly. 'It reminds me of very sharp teeth.'

Ignoring that, 'Your family isn't going to like this,' she warned him. 'Once they've recovered from their shock they're going to come down on you with every objection they can find.'

'Do I appear to give a damn?' He arched an eyebrow.

Her heart gave a flutter because—no, he didn't. 'I won't take a load of flak about the past,' she declared. 'If you bring it up, I'll walk, taking Rose with me and let you fight me for her through the courts.'

'What past?' he countered, filling her with a heady kind of heat because the man standing here wasn't thinking about anything but the length of her slender, silk-covered legs and how tightly they could grip him when he needed them to.

She uncrossed those legs and crossed them again slowly, sensually, and watched the flickering firelight catch hold of the gold flecks in his eyes.

'You provoking little witch.' He knew what she was doing.

'Sì,' she drawled unconscionably.

He moved like lightning. The glass she was cradling between her fingers disappeared. She was aided to her feet by two hands that circled her slender waist. His kiss devoured—*devoured*. Hunger, thirst, punishment, desire—you name it, he put it all into that one hot kiss.

'Let's go home,' he growled as he set her mouth free.

Reality arrived to give her an uncomfortable kick. Going 'home' as Luca called it meant going out there and facing the disapproval of his family.

'I'm—sorry,' she murmured, moving a step away from him.

'What for?' he asked.

'For falling apart when I was determined not to, and for causing that awful scene to happen at all.'

'The outcome of it was always going to happen,' he answered, then reached for her chin, lifted it so she had to look into his eyes. 'If you are carrying my child, we marry,' he stated flatly. 'If you are not carrying my child but you want to be a mother to Rose, then we marry. Either way—we marry.' He shrugged to declare that he'd covered it all.

'I am not carrying your child,' she stated adamantly.

Luca frowned. 'Why are you set against it?'

'I told you.' She tried to release her chin but he refused to let her, his long fingers simply moving to encompass one of her cheeks. 'I don't want to go through what Keira went through so many times.'

'Why do you fear that you will have the same problems?'

Her breasts shuddered on a small sigh. 'My mother died in childbirth,' she told him. 'How can I *not* expect it to be the same for me?'

'Because Keira did not die giving birth to Rose, she died because of a terrible freak accident.'

'And all of those dreadful disappointments she suffered year after year?' She shook her head, and still did not manage to dislodge his fingers and thumb. 'I know it must sound very cowardly, but I just can't put myself through that.'

'Did your mother have many miscarriages?'

'No,' she admitted. 'But she—'

'Then you are mixing two separate tragedies together here and frightening yourself with the results, so stop it,' he said quietly. 'Nothing is going to happen to you. If you are pregnant, then we will find you the best medical attention. If you are not and you really do continue to fear it, then Rose will be our only child—our special gift from Angelo and Keira.'

'Will that be enough for you?' Oh, she knew she sounded pathetically wistful, but his answer was so important to her.

'Idiota,' he chided, and pulled her towards him as he lowered his head and kissed her again but differently.

This kiss seemed to seal something, though what exactly, Shannon wasn't sure.

And the gauntlet of disapproval wasn't nearly as bad as she expected it to be, mainly because almost everyone but the immediate family had left while they'd been hiding in the library and as for the rest—well, Shannon had to assume that they knew what was in Angelo and Keira's will by now because there was an air of acceptance about their manner, which was marginally better than disapproval.

Luca's mother put it into words. 'This has been the worst week any of us could be forced to go through. It places everything that went before it in the shade. As Father Michael pointed out to us, our thoughts must be with Angelo and Keira's baby and I cannot think of two people who will love the child more than both of you will. Please, Shannon—can we make this day a fresh beginning for all of us instead of such an unhappy end?'

It was an olive branch she had never expected. It could have brought the tears flooding back if she hadn't glimpsed the cynical expression on Renata's face.

'Why is it that Father Michael has so much influence with your family?' she asked Luca as Fredo drove them away.

'Did you not know?' He turned a surprised frown on her. 'He is my uncle—my father's brother. Everyone in my family listens to him—even me, when I have to.'

They married a week later. Father Michael performed the ceremony. Luca pulled out all the stops and insisted she wear the frothiest wedding gown she could find. The fact that his motives were driven by the silly fuss she'd made about silver-framed pictures did not pass Shannon by.

The family was there to offer support. She was really surprised to discover that Renata's husband Tazio had offered to escort her down the aisle and that Sophia wanted to stand witness for her while Carlo did the honours for Luca.

Spreading it around, she mused hollowly as she stood beneath the stone archway with Luca at her side. Camera bulbs flashed. They were caught for posterity, though she felt no sense of belonging—yet.

It would come, though, she told herself determinedly. It had to do for Rose's sake if not for her own—and she had not placed all her future in Luca's hands without being prepared to fight tooth and nail to belong eventually.

She told Angelo and Keira that—quietly inside her head as she laid her bridal flowers on their grave.

They flew to London after the wedding. Shannon had a life to pack up and ship to Florence, including a job she had no intention of stopping because she had become a wife and was about to become a mother. She'd talked it over with Luca and they'd agreed that she could work from his apartment and commute to London when commitments made it necessary. So they'd also agreed to employ a nurse to help care for Rose, and even found the ideal candidate in one of the nurses at the hospital who'd been helping care for the baby since her birth. She'd grown so attached to Rose that she jumped at the chance of coming home with her when she was eventually allowed to leave the hospital. But that moment was a still few weeks away because Rose had to remain in her safe hospital environment until she had reached her proper birth date, which meant that Shannon had a few weeks' grace to get used to her new working regime and get organised for a baby before Rose and the nurse joined them.

Her business partner Joshua thought she was mad giving up everything to become a martyr to the Salvatores—as he saw it. But then, Joshua was a typical high-octane twenty-four-year-old with ambition shooting like steam from his ears. He could think of nothing worse than tying himself down to anything but his desire for success. It was when Luca pointed out to him that, with Shannon's fluent grasp of Italian and his own influential contacts, having her based in Florence could only be good for business. After that Joshua was almost packing up for her, he was that eager for her to get back to Florence. But, on a personal level, he was the closest friend she had in her life and he was concerned that she was going to be hurt badly again if she didn't take care.

She knew he was right, yet she was happy in an odd, quiet kind of way. She was letting herself love Luca and he couldn't be more supportive of her plans if he tried, though she didn't think love came into his reasons for pulling out all the stops in his effort to make this marriage work. And no one could make her question the passion they shared on a nightly basis in the luxurious surroundings of his London apartment or those other sensual interludes conducted while packing up her flat, where he was supposed to be helping but spent most of his time trying to get her out of her clothes.

No matter how she tried to she could not rid herself of the feeling that the bubble was going to burst at any second. But even thinking like that did not prepare her for the speed with which the bubble did burst.

It began five short days into their marriage. Luca received a call from his PA that resulted in him having to fly back to Florence immediately. Shannon hadn't finished packing up her flat so it meant he had to go back without her. He didn't like it—she didn't like it. Their marriage was too new and much too fragile for them to be risking a separation so soon. Before he left they made love as if they were never going to be together again and by the time he kissed her goodbye she was so close to changing her mind and going with him she was actually shocked as to how desperate she felt.

The next few days seemed to stretch out before her like an empty desert. She filled her time in by visiting her clients and soothing their concerns about her change in location. When she wasn't with clients she was packing and listening to Alex, her neighbour, wax enviously about the new life she was about to embark on with one of the sexiest men alive.

The sexiest man alive rang her each evening—and during the day if he could find the time. She missed him. She missed Rose and couldn't wait to get back to them.

Her things were shipped off to Florence by special courier. She was actually on the brink of booking her own flight there when the supermodel she'd met with in Paris called up to say that she would be in London in two days and wanted another meeting. It was too good an opportunity to pass up so she decided to stay a few days longer. Luca went on a cursing spree, then when he had calmed down he informed her that her things had arrived and she had better be following them soon or he would come and get her.

She liked the angry, possessive way he said that. It was all very nice, very float half an inch above ground. Nice place to be. She hugged the feeling to her as she went about her business the following day. Then it suddenly struck her that she hadn't done anything about proper contraception, so she made an appointment with her doctor with the happy idea that she could surprise Luca when she got back to Florence with the news that he wouldn't have to keep using the dreaded condoms he hated so much. The doctor was filling in a prescription slip when she thought to question him about whether it was safe to start taking pills when there was a small chance she might be pregnant.

'Well, let's find out,' he said.

CHAPTER EIGHT

LUCA rang that evening while Shannon was standing in the bedroom staring at the pale reflection in the dressing mirror that was hardly recognisable as her own face. Her phone was within fingertip reach and she answered with a wispy, 'Hi.'

'Hi yourself,' he echoed lazily. 'What are you doing?'

Falling apart, she thought. 'Nothing,' she answered. 'I've just got in. W-what about you?'

'I am still at the office. I have a few—things I need to do before I can leave. But doing nothing sounds inviting,' he then murmured, sounding husky and dark and gorgeously intimate. 'Maybe we could do this nothing together. Would an interlude of telephone sex appeal to you?'

Shannon watched long, mascara-tipped lashes folding down over sapphire blue eyes then lifting up again. 'Not right now,' she refused. 'I'm—' falling apart '—about to take a shower,' she improvised hazily.

'Well, if that image does not encourage telephone sex then I am in a worse state than I thought.' He laughed. 'Are you undressed already? If so you are going to have to wait while I play catch-up.'

'N-no.' She watched her eyes blink again. 'I've just got in.'

'You've already told me that.' There was a moment of silence, a hint of tension suddenly whipping down the line, then— 'Are you all right, *cara*?' he asked.

'Fine,' she said.

'You don't sound fine.'

And he no longer sounded husky, she realised, and made

herself turn her back to the mirror so she could try to concentrate. 'Sorry,' she said. 'I've had a—rough day.'

'Doing what?'

Did she tell him—cold like this via a telephone? 'I…' A hand went up to cover her forehead, confusion and shock making it impossible to think. 'I w-went shopping, bought too much then—' she couldn't tell him, not like this '—then couldn't remember where I parked m-my car.'

'You sold your car last week,' he reminded her softly and there was no gentleness in that soft tone. He was becoming cross and suspicious of this whole crazy conversation.

Pull yourself together! she told herself tautly, and heaved some air into her lungs and managed to make it sound like a laugh as it left her again. 'I know. Isn't that stupid? I shopped till I dropped then went looking for a car I don't even have any more!' Swinging away from her own lies, she walked on shaking legs over to the bed. 'See what you've done to me?' she said as she sat down. 'I'm losing my mind and it has to be your fault because I was absolutely fine before you came back into my life.'

'So, I make you lose your mind, that's OK. I can live with that,' he accepted quietly. 'Now tell what's really wrong?'

He wasn't taking the bait. She felt the tears start to press at the back of her eyes. 'I have a headache,' she quavered honestly.

'Ah, the classic headache,' his mocking sigh whispered into her ear. 'No wonder you don't want telephone sex with me.'

The diversion had worked—he was sounding husky again. She liked husky, it squeezed tightly at her heart but she still liked it. 'I'm missing you,' she added for good measure. 'And I'm missing Rose. Have you seen her today?'

'We spent the afternoon together, and we missed you too,' Luca returned still frowning because that instinct he possessed where Shannon was concerned was telling him she still had not told him what was really upsetting her. 'She has changed so much in a week that you won't know her, I promise you. She has her mama's eyes and—' He stopped when he caught the sound of movement. 'Would you prefer it if I called back later when you've had your shower and you feel—?'

'No!' she protested. 'I l-like listening to your voice.'

'While doing what?' he asked. 'I can hear you moving around.'

'I'm making myself comfortable on the bed,' she told him as she crawled up the bed and curled up on his pillow.

'Wouldn't you rather I go so you can—?'

'No!' she responded. 'Tell me more about Rose,' she encouraged.

So he did in low-toned, husky Italian, while Shannon listened with the phone tucked between the pillow and her ear and for extra comfort tugged another pillow towards her so she could hug it as if it were him.

While Luca reclined in his chair behind his desk in his office and wondered what was really troubling her, because something certainly was.

Was it grief? Had he caught her at a bad moment when she had been thinking of her sister? Hell, why not? he thought. Hadn't he been sitting here thinking about Angelo and the gut-wrenching task that lay ahead of him this evening when he eventually found the courage to enter his brother's office to begin clearing it out?

His gut gave him a thick thump just by his thinking about it. 'You've gone quiet,' he said huskily when he realised that her muffled little responses had faded away. 'Are you asleep?'

'Almost,' her whispered response trailed into his ear and down through his body like a lover's caress.

He sat forward, reaching out to pick up the bunch of keys

that had been sitting on his desk staring at him for the last few hours. 'I will let you go, then,' he murmured, deciding it was time that he got the deed done with.

'OK,' she said, but she didn't sound happy about it, which made him smile.

'I will call again in the morning.'

'Early,' she told him and his smile became a rueful grin. 'I...miss you...' she added.

And the grin faded when his heart turned over and squeezed painfully because *miss you* wasn't enough. He wanted to hear *I love you Luca*, in that same soft, serious tone she used to use to say those words to him.

'I miss you too.' The keys bit into his palm as he clenched his fingers around them because he knew he couldn't say it either, though he wanted to.

The call ended. He sat staring at his cell-phone while a bleak feeling of dissatisfaction gnawed its way into his senses, tempting him to call her back and just say the damn words and get it over with. But how did he do it? How did a man admit he was still in love with the same woman who had betrayed him two years ago?

He didn't, was the easy answer—and he stood up abruptly, then turned the phone off altogether just to make a point. Angry, fed up and frustrated with himself, he shifted his attention to the bunch of keys in his other hand and on a few tight, self-aimed curses stepped around his desk and headed for the door that linked his brother's office to his.

He didn't call.

After spending a sleepless night tossing and turning, counting off the minutes and the hours until she would hear his voice again, Shannon didn't know if she was hurt or angry that he had not bothered with the promised early morning call.

So she tried calling him, only to discover that his phone was switched off. Had he let the battery run down? she wondered, and refused to listen to the little voice in her head reminding her that he had several spare batteries to cover such an eventuality, because the idea of a flat battery was a more acceptable reason for him not calling her than him just forgetting to do it.

By twelve o'clock she was fretting because he still hadn't called, and when she tried his number she received the same automated message telling her the telephone she was trying to connect to was not available, which also forced her to acknowledge that her flat-battery theory was stupid so—where was he? What was he doing that was so important it would make him switch off his phone?

A leap of panic had her ringing the hospital in Florence in case Rose had taken ill. Nerves rattling, heart racing, she listened to a nurse reassuring her that the baby was fine but, no, Signor Salvatore had not been in to visit the baby as yet that day.

At two o'clock she attended her meeting with the super-model, determined to hang onto her professional persona even though she wanted to jump up and down and shout or fall apart as she usually did in times of crisis.

An hour later she was standing in a street somewhere in Mayfair, with a new contract secured and due to meet Joshua at their offices to bring him up to scratch about the contract before they headed off to their local wine bar to celebrate.

But she didn't do anything. She just stood in that cold Mayfair street and called Luca's number again. When there was still no response, she began calling every number in Florence she had logged in her phone in an effort to track him down. He wasn't answering at the apartment. She'd tried his office, his mother, even both of his sisters to no avail. No one seemed to know where he was or why he was not contactable. Everyone was as bewildered as she.

And she needed—*needed* to talk to him!

She hit the panic button. She didn't know why she had to hit it at that precise moment standing in a busy street, but before she knew it she'd made the decision and was in a taxi and heading directly for Heathrow.

She managed to get a seat on a flight into Pisa leaving within the hour and only then had the sense to check if she had her passport with her and was relieved to find it still stashed in her bag from the last time she'd used it.

'What do you mean, you're on the way to Florence?' Joshua shouted at her down the phone. 'We have a surprise farewell party waiting here for you!'

'I'm s-sorry,' she apologised. 'Tell everyone I'm sorry. But I have to go, Josh, it's important.'

'You mean *he's* important.'

Oh, yes, she thought. I just didn't realise how much until I couldn't reach him. 'I can't get in touch with him and I'm—scared.'

It reminded her of the last time he'd done this to her. The same thick clutch of anxiety was dragging her aching heart around her insides as if looking for somewhere to hide from what his silence had to mean.

'This is different, Shannon.' Joshua toned down his anger when he heard the anxious quiver in her voice. 'You managed to sort out your old differences and you're *married* to him.'

But they hadn't sorted anything out. They'd merely agreed to put it all on a shelf marked 'pending'.

'When did you last speak?'

'Last night.'

'Last night?' Joshua choked. 'For goodness' sake, Shannon, how often is a busy man like Luca Salvatore supposed to contact his wife to keep her happy? You're going over the top here, sweetheart,' he told her bluntly. 'Take a deep breath and calm down, then remind me not to get myself stuck in the marriage trap if this is the kind of hassle I will have to look forward to.'

She laughed. Josh was right. She took that deep breath. Her silly, stupid nerves began to calm down. 'Thanks,' she said.

'Don't mention it,' Joshua drawled. 'Now, are you going to revert to your original plan to fly out to Florence tomorrow and come back here for a booze-up with your brethren?'

'No,' she said and felt her anxieties erupt again. 'I still have something to tell him that can't wait.'

'Don't tell me, let me guess,' Joshua sighed. 'You've got to fly a million miles just to say *I love you, Luca*!'

'One day you're going to meet your own Waterloo, Joshua, and I want a front seat when it happens,' she snapped at his sarcasm.

'Am I right?' he challenged.

'No,' she said and glanced at her watch. Her flight was about to be called. 'I'm going to tell him that I'm pregnant with his child.'

She cut the connection before Joshua could blurt out his response to that announcement, then just stood staring at the waves of people flowing through the airport, stunned by what she was feeling now she'd let herself say the words out loud.

Fear mainly, mixed with a stammering sense of excitement that was threatening to make her legs give out. She made for her departure gate before it happened, took her seat on the plane in a mindless daze.

It was dark when she landed in Pisa. From there she had to catch the train into Florence, then hire a taxi to take her the rest of the way.

And in all of that time and travel, Luca still had not tried to contact her cell-phone. Joshua might think she was being silly expecting him to, but she didn't. In fact silly didn't even touch what she was feeling. Angry, hurt, indignant—

offended better described what was fizzing inside her as she rode the lift up to Luca's apartment.

The first thing she saw when she stepped out of the lift was her packing cases stacked up against a wall. The daunting task of having to unpack them all again brought her to a halt for a few seconds while she allowed herself a silent groan.

Then she moved off through the arch looking for Luca without holding out much hope of finding him here, since she'd rung and rung here only to have the answering service take over each time.

So it came as a shock to throw open the sitting room door and find what she did. The room looked as if a bomb had been dropped on it; papers and documents were strewn everywhere. But it was the sight of Luca stretched out on one of the sofas that held her frozen. He was wearing the trousers to one of his dark suits and a wine red shirt tugged open at his throat. His shoes were missing, his jacket, his tie, and even as the smell of hard alcohol assailed her nostrils she saw a squat glass half filled with something golden he had slotted between a set of long fingers and the half-empty bottle of whisky standing on the low table an arms reach away from him.

Every picture tells a story, Shannon thought grimly. And this one told her that he was asleep—lost in a drunken stupor, she suspected indignantly—the glass moving up and down with the rhythm of his deep breathing where it rested on his chest!

While she had been worrying herself out of her head about him, rushing to catch planes *and* letting down all her work colleagues—Luca been right here enjoying his own private boozing party!

Her eyes took on a murderous glitter. Taking a sharp step forward, she lifted a hand and sent the door into its housing with a very satisfying crash.

Luca jolted like a man shot, opened his eyes and through a bleary haze of alcohol saw her standing there. For a full ten seconds he couldn't move a single muscle, wondering if he had conjured her up from the deepest, darkest nightmare he had ever had in his life.

'So this is why no one can get hold of you!' Her voice lashed itself against his fragile senses.

'Madre de Dio,' he groaned and rolled into a sitting position. 'What are you doing here?' he demanded bemusedly. 'Have I lost a whole day?'

'Try switching on your phone, then you would know,' she snapped. 'And I think it's more important that you explain what the heck you think you're doing here?'

'Don't shout,' he groaned, making a grab for his aching head.

'Don't shout?' she repeated, her voice lifting a full octave. 'I've just flown halfway across Europe worrying why I can't get in touch with you and I find you happily ensconced in here rolling drunk! Why shouldn't I shout?'

'I was not expecting you—all right?' he uttered thickly as her decibels played havoc with his head.

'That makes it OK?' She wasn't impressed. 'I married a closet drunk, is that it? And what are all these papers doing scattered about the—'

She stopped suddenly. Luca felt his blood turn from pure malt whisky to ice. Lowering his hand from his eyes, he was just in time to see her start to bend to pick up a piece of paper. 'No,' he rasped. 'Don't—' and leapt to his feet.

But he was too late. Shannon already had the notepaper in her trembling fingers. Her heart began to pump unevenly. She tried to take a breath and found that she couldn't. She knew this notepaper. Her mouth ran dry, her eyes beginning to sting as she looked around her and saw more of the same scattered about.

Then she noticed the others that were not quite the same but she still recognised them.

'What have you done?' She began darting round the room picking up the papers as a heaving ball of agony built in her chest. 'Why have you got these?'

These being Keira's letters to her—Keira's *private* letters! And not just Keira's letters to her that she'd had safely stored away in a packing case, but her letters to Keira were here too!

'You've been through my private papers.' She didn't want to believe it. 'You must have gone through Keira's as well!' She lifted her head to look at him and went pale when she saw the expression on his face.

He didn't even look guilty, but hard and angry. 'How could you?' she whispered.

'But they made such a revealing read,' he said bitterly. 'All that begging you did before your tone turned to ice.'

Then he took a gulp at his whisky when she flinched.

'Y-you sh-shouldn't have read them.' She was shaking so badly she could barely get the words out. 'They w-were not yours to read.'

'Do you mean the one where she begs you not to tell me about what she'd done because I would have to tell Angelo?' he threw back. 'Or the one where she promises you *faithfully* that she will never do such a wicked thing again!'

Oh, dear God. Shannon swallowed across a throat that was paper-dry suddenly. 'Sh-she was afraid of losing him.'

'My besotted brother? He would have forgiven her if she'd taken her lover to his *own* damn bed!'

This time when she flinched he swung his back to her. Shannon could see the angry muscles flexing across his shoulders as he took another pull on his drink. Her head was buzzing, and she was trembling so badly that she only just made it to the nearest chair before her legs gave out.

'Sitting ducks,' Luca muttered.

Still lost in a shocked daze, 'I b-beg your pardon?' she said.

'Angelo and me,' he enlightened. 'A pair of sitting ducks for a pair of lethal witches.' He uttered a hard laugh. Everything about his was hard from the iron-cast profile to the tightly clenched angry stance.

'Now hold on a minute.' She pushed out a protest. 'Don't use that derisive tone on me because I don't recall you forgiving me for my so-called sins, Luca.'

'You should have told me the truth.'

'I *tried* telling you the truth but you refused to believe me!'

'Not then—*now*!' He swung on her harshly. '*This* time around!'

'Why would I want to tarnish the memory of a beautiful person whose only fault was she needed to be loved too much by too many people?'

It was his turn to go white. 'You mean the man she took to our bed was not the *only* one?'

'Yes, he was the only one!' She jumped up furiously. 'She adored Angelo—you know that she did! But their marriage was in trouble,' she tagged on reluctantly, and began pacing the floor while staring at the letters still clutched in her fingers because she couldn't stay still and look at Luca while she talked about this. 'Angelo was fed up with performing according to calendars and menstrual cycles so he s-stopped coming home every night. Keira decided he didn't love her any more so when some guy came along and showed her she was still lovable, she fell for his silver-tongued charm like a brick.'

'How do you know all of this?' If Luca had been pale before, he was a grey colour now. 'None of what you have just said is in those letters.'

'It was happening while I was here living with you.' She turned, to find his face had blurred now, and knew she was about to give way to tears. 'Didn't you notice that those six months must have been the only months my sister wasn't pregnant at some stage?' she questioned unevenly. 'Or that Angelo was working incredibly long hours every day?'

'We were in the middle of some big company changes,' he dismissed impatiently.

'You still managed to come home to me every night.'

'Are you suggesting that Angelo was going to someone else?' he barked out furiously.

'I wouldn't have a clue!' she cried. 'The important point here is that Keira believed that he was!'

'And you knew she was feeling like this and did not bother to bring her concerns to me?'

Which brought them right back full circle, Shannon noted heavily—but she still lifted her chin, eyes tear-bright as she challenged him. 'If Angelo had been having an affair and you knew about it, would you have told me?'

He stared at her for a moment, then turned away, his answer lying in the thick silence that clattered down around the two of them. Sibling loyalty was the pits when it encroached on your own life, Shannon thought painfully.

'I'll be honest,' she dropped into that silence. 'I was selfish. I was madly, madly in love and so happy I didn't want to think about anyone else but you and me. So I told Keira not to be silly and more or less left her with no one to turn to for—' Her voice broke; she struggled to recover it. '*Why* did you have to bring all of this up again?' she choked out. 'She didn't even do anything! Can you believe that? I'd gone to London to pack up my life there, then missed you so much that I came back early—hey,' she mocked then, '*déjà vu*!' and swallowed hard on the next lumps of tears to grab at her aching throat. 'You were supposed to be in...' She couldn't remember.

'Milan,' he provided.

She nodded, pressed her trembling lips together in an effort to control them then grimly forced herself to go on. 'I came back to your apartment to find this strange man in our bed and a scantily dressed Keira standing beside it tugging at the sheets and sobbing at him to get up and get dressed because she couldn't do it.' The scene could still set her senses reeling with horror and shock. 'Th-then they saw me standing there and Keira ran and locked herself in the bathroom leaving me to tell the guy to get the hell out. By the time you arrived, I'd got the whole story out of her and sent her home with the promise that I wouldn't tell a soul so long as she never did such a stupid thing again!'

'You don't need to go on,' he put in thickly.

'No,' she agreed and began to shiver so badly she had to hug herself. 'But you tell me what I was supposed to do next, Luca?' she demanded. 'Because I still don't have an answer to that!'

'You still should have told me.'

Shannon almost stamped a foot in frustration. 'I did!' she cried. 'You refused to believe me!'

'Once!' He swung around to scorn that. He looked pale and hard and tough and cold. She shivered again. 'You mentioned her name *once* before it was quickly withdrawn again!'

'Because you almost took my head off!'

'I think I'm going to do it now,' he gritted and actually took a step towards her before he pulled himself up with an angry hiss that rattled with fury. 'This is going nowhere,' he uttered.

He was right and it wasn't. She felt sick and hurt and angry and bitter, and he looked like the cold, dark stranger who'd walked into her flat several weeks ago. Where had all the new tender warmth gone? Why did it always have to be other people's problems that tore them to shreds like this? Maybe because they never should have come together in the first place, she answered her own bleak question.

Maybe it was fate's way of saying—Get out of each other's lives, for goodness' sake. You don't belong together.

When you went straight to the bottom line what did they have worthy of keeping them together? 'Great sex,' she muttered, that was all.

'Cosa?'

'You and me and going nowhere,' she enlightened dully. 'We have great sex and nothing else really.'

It was his turn to flinch. 'There is more to this relationship than what takes place between the sheets,' he insisted.

Was there? Shannon stared down at the letters trembling in her hands and thought about that statement. 'You married me because you thought you had no other option,' she told him. 'You did it for Rose's sake, *and* because of the great sex! But most of all, Luca, I think you married me because you needed to be sure you kept some control over who controlled me and my say over Angelo's heavy stock share in the Salvatore empire.'

'That is utter rubbish,' he discarded.

'Is it? Then why did you feel you had to go through my private letters?' she challenged. 'You had to be looking for something important to do such a wicked thing! Did you hope to find something to use against me in court if this stupid marriage didn't work? Proof about my ill-gotten life-style, maybe, that would say I was an unfit mother for Rose and totally unfit to be a co-guardian of her inheritance!'

'Madre de dio,' he breathed. 'I do not believe this. You could not be more wrong!' he charged.

But Shannon wasn't listening. She had suddenly spied another letter lying half hidden beneath a chair and made a dive for it. It was one of her letters to Keira. Tears flooded into her eyes.

'How could you?' she choked, kneeling on the floor and attempting to sift the letters into some kind of order on her lap while her fingers shook and her eyes burned. 'How could you go to her house and hunt through Keira's private papers like a—'

'I didn't,' he sighed.

She looked up. 'Didn't what?'

'Did not go to Angelo and Keira's house.' He put it in plainer words. 'I have not been there since…'

He couldn't bring himself to say it; instead he uttered a thick curse and sank back onto the sofa, dropped the glass onto the low table, then bent over to scrape long fingers through his hair.

'Then how did you get your hands on her letters?' she demanded.

Luca covered his face with his hands and wished the alcohol had done its job and completely numbed his brain. He didn't want to think; he didn't want to look at what he'd been doing last night, or what the future was going to mean now he'd discovered what he had.

'I was clearing Angelo's desk out in his office,' he told her. 'The letters were hidden at the back of a drawer…'

'Oh, dear God,' Shannon breathed, and he knew she'd already leapt ahead of him to the next part as this bleak, miserable mess began to unfold.

'I don't know how long Angelo had known about them or if Keira knew that he had them at all,' he pushed on, spelling it out for her anyway. 'But the fact is that my brother knew the truth about what happened two years ago, yet he could not bring himself to come and tell me.'

And there was the reason for the angrily scattered letters and his whisky binge, he admitted heavily. Not only had he discovered the truth about two years ago, but he had also realised that the brother he loved had kept from him the one thing Angelo of all people had known was important to him.

Shannon was innocent.

'I have spent the last two years believing I had the right to hate you with every damn day that went by,' he ground out huskily. 'Huh, what a joke. It was me that let you down, and my own brother could not tell me that!'

'He was protecting Keira.'

For some reason that remark shot sparks down his backbone. 'And that makes it OK?'

'No,' she admitted. 'But Angelo and Keira are no longer here to defend themselves, so I can't see the use in raking over it all again.'

'I refused to believe you—make me defend that!'

She sighed and got up. 'Can you defend it?'

'*You* should have told me—showed me those letters. You owed it to me.'

'Ah, so it's my fault. Good defence,' she commended.

'I did not mean that.'

'Then what did you mean?'

'I don't know, damn it!' he snapped and picked up his drink.

'Any more of that stuff and you'll fall over the next time you stand up,' she said tartly and started walking towards the door.

The glass was slammed back down on the table. It was amazing how quickly a man the size of Luca could move when he was provoked enough, Shannon noted as he swung to his feet and rounded the sofa and was standing over her before she'd even blinked. His hands grabbed her shoulders, the next thing she knew she was being pinned against the nearest wall.

'Very macho,' she murmured, but she was trembling again.

'I won't let you leave me,' he bit out thinly.

'I didn't say I was going to.' She frowned.

'You can hate me for the rest of our lives but you will do it right here, where I can see you doing it.'

His eyes were so black she felt as if she were falling into them, his hands possessive, his mouth tensely parted but gorgeous with it, and his breath so loaded with whisky fumes that they began to go to her head. 'OK,' she agreed hazily.

Frustration raked across his features. 'Take me seriously,' he snapped.

'I've only just got here!' she shot back at him. 'Why the heck are you expecting me to leave again?'

'You were going to the door.' Now he was trembling.

'To put these letters away with my other things!' she cried.

'You should be stuffing them down my disbelieving throat!'

She went one better, caught her bottom lip in her teeth and aimed the flat of her other hand at the side of his face. She didn't know where it came from but for some stupid reason the tears were back in her eyes. 'That's for going through my private possessions,' she heaved out shakily as her finger marks drew lines on his cheek. 'And if I h-had the strength left I w-would hit you again for upsetting me when I was already upset before I got here!'

'Why were you upset?'

'I'm—pregnant,' she whispered and watched as all that domineering macho anger turned into a block of stone. He didn't even swallow. In fact he didn't do anything.

'S-say something,' she stammered, then did something herself. Her vision went funny, all woozy and washy. She closed her eyes and knew she was going to faint.

'Shannon…?' was the last hoarse word she heard uttered before everything went black.

Luca cursed and caught her to him as she began to slide down the wall. Then he kept on cursing as he gathered her into his arms and turned to carry her to one of the sofas. She looked like death and he wanted to hit something—himself preferably.

Pregnant—

For a couple of seconds he seriously thought he was going to join her in her get-out swoon. Then concern for her took over—a concern that should have *always* been hers!

Dio, he hated himself. He was the worst kind of man a woman would want in her life—one that did not believe her and did not trust her and made her pregnant when it was what she feared the most!

'Shannon…' He called her name but she made no response to it.

Twisting his body, he dipped his fingers in the whisky glass, then turned back to moisten her bloodless lips with it. She was so limp and lifeless his skin began to prickle. Getting up, he went to get his cell-phone from his jacket pocket. The moment he switched it on half a dozen messages popped up on the screen. He'd intended to use the phone to call for a doctor but for some crazy reason he found himself opening text messages.

'I need to talk to you. Shannon.'

'Where are you? Shannon.'

'I'm coming to Florence. Shannon.'

'I'm frightened. Please call me. Shannon.'

'Why won't you speak to me? Shannon.'

He couldn't even swallow.

'I need to hear your voice, Luca!'

'Luca—'

His attention reeled back to the owner of those pitiful messages, lying there on the sofa with a slender white hand now covering her mouth.

'I think I'm going to be sick,' she whispered frailly.

CHAPTER NINE

LUCA leapt at Shannon, tossing the cell-phone aside to gather her back into his arms.

'I don't believe you sometimes,' he gritted as he made for the door with her head resting on his shoulder and his husky voice rumbling against her cheek. 'I suppose you flew all of this way without taking on refreshment again? When will you learn to be sensible? Last time it was cramp, this time you faint and now you feel sick. If you had waited until tomorrow my plane would have delivered you here in comfort. Why do you always have to mess up my plans? I am smashed out of my head and I cannot think straight. What man wants his woman to catch him like this?'

'Wife,' Shannon mumbled.

He pulled to a stop in the hallway, mind locked on the single word as if it were alien to him. Then his chest heaved.

'Sì,' he confirmed and started moving again, shouldering his way through the bedroom door, then making straight for the bathroom where she was noisily, humiliatingly sick into the toilet while he squatted behind her holding back her hair and spitting out curses that sang in her head.

By the time it was over it was all she could do to sink weakly against him. Her head was swimming; his curses still echoed in her head. She was trembling and shivering on the aftermath of her nausea, her skin felt clammy and the last thing she needed right then was for him to move her again. He picked her up, flushed the toilet, then slammed down the seat so he could sit down on it with her still wrapped in his arms. Muscles began flexing all over him as he stretched out a hand towards the washbasin and just managed to reach a tap and turn it on. Two seconds later a damp cloth arrived on her face. It was so refreshing she just closed her eyes and gave in to his grimly silent ministrations with the back of her head resting in the hollow of his shoulder and her legs dangling limply along the length of his.

Eventually he went still. Her world began to steady. She could feel the pound of his heart against the back of her head. The whole urgent shift from sofa to bathroom could not have taken more than two minutes yet she felt as if she'd just climbed Mount Everest and had a suspicion that he felt the same.

She released a small sigh.

'Feeling a little better?'

'Mmm,' She became aware that her hair was plastered across the front of his shirt. She lifted a weak hand with the intention of gathering the long, straight strands together—but Luca caught the hand and held onto it. The next thing she knew he was lifting it to his lips.

'Forgive me,' he murmured.

'What for?' she sighed.

'Not listening to you and believing in you when I should have done.'

'It looked bad. I knew that.'

'But I should have given you a fair hearing,' he insisted. 'I should not have—'

'You promised me that we wouldn't do this, Luca,' she snapped out suddenly, wriggling her fingers free and finding the strength to stand on her own two feet. 'No raking up the past, we said.'

'I did not know what I know now when we agreed to that.'

'But I did,' she said, using angry fingers to hunt out a tube of toothpaste and a toothbrush. 'What has changed for me other than you now know the truth?'

'Everything has changed for me.' He stood up, restless now, angry and tense.

'And you can't live with that?'

'Not right now—no,' he replied and walked out of the bathroom.

Shannon stood with the toothbrush loaded with toothpaste and listened tensely for him to leave the bedroom. If he does I'm finished with him, she told herself fiercely. If he walks away from this, I am out of here and booking into a hotel!

The toothbrush went into her mouth. She glared at her own washed out reflection in the bathroom mirror while she scrubbed at her teeth. Her hair was a mess, full of strand-tangling static, and if she'd started out today looking good enough to make the supermodel scowl again then she certainly did not look like that now!

It was easier to look away—better to look away because the bedroom door still hadn't slammed to mark his exit and the sheer tension in waiting for it to happen was making her tremble again. She turned on the cold tap, angrily cleaned her toothbrush, then bent to rinse out her mouth. The moment she lowered her head a fresh wave of dizziness set the floor rocking beneath her feet, forcing her to cling to the washbasin or fall in a jelly-legged heap. 'Oh,' she sobbed out in angry frustration. This just wasn't fair!

A strong arm hooked around her waist to take her weight again. The toothbrush was snatched away. He didn't even curse this time, but simmered in magnificent silence as he bent to hook the other arm around her knees then carried her out of the bathroom with his profile set in iron again.

'You're doing a lot of hefting and carrying for a drunk,' she remarked acidly.

'Discovering that my wife is pregnant has a way of sobering me up.' He deposited her on the edge of the bed.

'Oh.' She'd forgotten she'd told him that. 'Do you mind?' she asked warily.

'Do *I* mind?' He released a hard laugh and got down on

his haunches and began undoing the buttons on her jacket. 'You find out you are pregnant. You get so scared that you cannot even bring yourself to tell me when I call you last night.' The jacket came off. 'So we have this strange conversation where I think as if I am helping you through a lonely period of grieving for your sister—'

'I grieve all the time.'

'I am aware of that—so do I!' he snapped, pulling her jumper off over her head and making her hair crackle with static. 'But last night you were scared, and I *felt* your fear.' The flat of his palms tamed her hair. 'You should have told me what was worrying you and I would have flown straight back to London to be there for you.'

He started on the zips to her boots next. 'I know,' she said.

'Then why didn't you tell me?'

'Because it isn't something you tell someone over the telephone,' she answered defensively. 'I wanted to tell you properly—face to face.'

'But I ruined that for you too.' The boots came off. He stared at her feet. 'You're wearing my socks,' he sighed.

Shannon wriggled her toes. 'Another illusion shattered.' She smiled. 'I don't sleep around. I don't tell you all my secrets. I wear men's socks underneath my boots.'

There was an earthy, frustrated animal growl as he reared up to his full height. 'How can you joke about this?' he demanded.

'What do you want me to do?' she flared up at him. 'Fall into a fit of screaming hysterics instead? OK.' She jumped up to face him furiously. 'I'm pregnant when I don't want to be pregnant and it's all your fault!'

Her dreadful accusation hung in the silence. 'I'm sorry,' she burst out in anxious remorse. 'I didn't mean—'

He spun on his heels and walked away—out of the bedroom altogether this time, and he didn't even slam the door.

She wished he had. She wished he'd yelled back at her then flattened her on the bed! What she'd said wasn't even true because she did want this baby! She was just so terribly scared of what lay ahead of her.

'Oh, damn—*damn*!' she bit out angrily and turned back to the bathroom with the decision to lose herself in the shower in the vague hope it would ease away some of the awful stress. By the time she'd walked into the bathroom she had changed her mind in favour of a long soak in a warm scented bath.

Or maybe the bath was a delaying tactic before she had to go out there and face Luca again because she knew she had some serious apologising to do for that final remark and she had never been very good at apologising to him.

An image of that cold-eyed look he'd sent her before he'd walked out jumped up to hit her conscience again. Her lower stomach quivered.

'Don't you start,' she muttered. 'You're too tiny to have an opinion.'

Then she realised who it was she was talking to and a different kind of quiver ran through her. 'Oh, God,' she sighed. I am in such an emotional mess.

Piling her hair up on top of her head, she stripped away the rest of her clothes then stepped into the bath. As the warm, silky water closed around her she tried very hard to relax and put everything else out of her head.

It worked—in a fashion. A whole, long, uninterrupted hour later, bathed, dressed in her blue pyjamas with the matching wrap and smelling of sweet-scented bath oils, she let herself out of the bedroom and padded on bare feet to the kitchen in search of something to eat. She still felt a bit shaky but the nausea had receded, leaving her stomach growling for food.

The kitchen was in darkness. No sign of Luca, but for now she was glad about that. Flicking on the light switch she went to put the kettle to boil, then turned to open the refrigerator door to see what there was to eat.

Nothing she fancied eating, she realised as she gazed at the unappetising fridgy type things that got left in there because nobody wanted them. There was a wedge of cheese—was she allowed cheese in her condition? There were eggs—was she allowed eggs? She didn't even know if she was allowed to drink the milk—was it pasteurised or unpasteurised that was bad for pregnant women?

Sighing, she gave up and walked out of the kitchen, crossed the hall and walked into the sitting room. It had been cleaned up since she'd been carried from it, she noticed. No sign of the whisky bottle, but the letters lay neatly stacked on the table. The traitors, she thought, then made herself turn to where her senses were telling her Luca stood, staring out of the window at the dark night.

He'd changed his clothes for a pair of dark grey trousers and casual black sweater that finished at his waist. His hands were lost in his trouser pockets and there was something about the way he was standing there that made him look lonely and bleak and about as remote as he could do.

'I'm—sorry,' she burst out anxiously. 'I really didn't mean to heap all the blame onto you. It's just that I'm—'

'Frightened,' he put in for her.

But he didn't turn to look at her as he said it, and there wasn't a single muscle on him anywhere that so much as flexed. Another clutch of remorse played havoc with her conscience and she knew she was going to have to do a bit more than utter an apology if she was ever going to feel comfortable with herself again.

They needed physical contact and lots of it.

Luca watched her come towards him via her reflection in the darkened glass. Her hair was piled up on top of her head and she was wearing the blue pyjamas. Her face had a scrubbed clean look to it but it also wore the strain of the last twenty-four hours.

If she touched him he'd had it. If she uttered one small damned unfair feminine sob then he promised himself he was going to turn and toss her onto the nearest sofa and slake all of this bloody *guilt* burning inside him with a hard hot session of lust.

She had no right to look so beautiful. She had no right to look so delicate and frail. She was pregnant with his child. An odd sensation skittered down his torso and gathered in his crotch. He wanted to turn and wrap her in his arms and promise her that he would make sure everything was fine for her. He wanted to pick her up and carry her back to bed and *show* her how much he meant it, but—

Was it safe for them to make love in her delicate condition?

Was it safe for Shannon to have his baby at all?

That odd sensation in his crotch dissipated then regrouped to turn itself back into pangs of guilt. She was innocent of all charges two years ago. She had married him knowing he'd still believed she'd cheated on him. Why had she done that? What made this beautiful woman tick inside if she was prepared to throw her life away on a no good cynic like him, not once, but twice!

She disappeared out of his field of vision, his throat closed because he knew what was coming next. She was going to touch him. She was going to try to make amends when it should be him making those amends.

Her hands arrived first, sliding around his waist. He watched them via the window reflection begin travelling up the wall of his stomach until they came to rest against his chest. He *felt* them arrive and had to close his eyes as her cheek came to rest against his back.

'I'm hungry,' she mumbled sulkily, 'and there's nothing to eat in the fridge.'

'If you had come back tomorrow as planned we would have a full stock of fresh provisions,' he responded coolly.

A new silence fell. He felt her stiffen a little, opened his eyes to watch the crescents of her nails curl to dig into his flesh. 'A bigger man would take pity and let me off the hook now,' she told him.

A bigger man would not have to retract his fingers into fists in his pockets so they couldn't follow the hardening rise of his sex, he thought dryly.

And a bigger man would turn and take her in his arms, then tell her how much he loved her—without bringing in the sex. But his chance to say those words to her had come and gone the night before during a long telephone conversation when words like I love you would have meant something because he had not known then what he now knew.

So what did he do? Keep his earlier promise to himself and throw her down on the nearest sofa, or did he go for the big one, say the damn words to get it over with, then see what the hell he got back?

Shannon could feel his heart pounding; she could feel the way he was holding every muscle taut like a barrier against her. And he didn't say a single word.

It was rejection of the worst kind. A rejection she just hadn't anticipated so it had the capacity to hurt all the more. Now she didn't know what to do, didn't know how to pull away from him and keep her dignity at the same time.

Then she thought, Oh, just do it! and slid her hands away, then took a step back.

Luca realised he'd left too long a gap without responding the moment she stepped back from him. By the time he'd had the sense to turn to look at her she was already walking back to the door.

'Come back here,' he growled impatiently. 'I was about to suggest I order food in from the restaurant down the street.'

'I'll make a sandwich,' she said and kept on going.

'Don't be so stubborn, damn it,' he exploded. 'Just tell me what you would like and I will order it!'

Shannon paused in the doorway to glance back at him, and discovered that he'd decided to turn and face her at last. The lamplight was catching the damp gloss of his hair now and his skin had recovered some of its warm golden glow. He was so handsome, she thought achingly. So much her kind of man that even when he played the arrogant bastard she still loved him more than he deserved.

'I'll have pizza, then,' she said. 'Thank you.' It was a very prim little thank you that gave her time to watch his top lip give a twitch of distaste before she turned away. The Luca Salvatores of this world never ate pizza. To them it was an insult to Italian cuisine.

She wandered back into the kitchen with a twitch to her mouth that was pure wicked amusement. The kettle was just coming to the boil as she entered. She went to reach up for the coffee beans, then suddenly stopped again.

Was she allowed coffee?

Was she allowed tea?'

Pregnant.

That frisson ran through her again. It happened each time she let herself so much as *think* that word. It was scary but exciting but scary—

The kitchen door swung open and Luca strode in. He kept right on going through to the utility room where he kept his racks of wine.

'Red or white?' he called.

Was she allowed wine?

She didn't reply.

He came to lean in the doorway with his dark eyes hooded and a sardonic tilt to his mouth. He was waiting for an answer. She refused to look at him.

'I'll just have water, I think,' she said and reached for the loaf of crusty Italian bread sitting on the counter and began hacking at it with a bread knife.

The silence came back. They were becoming really good at dragging out the tension without uttering a single word, she noted as he continued to stand there trying to outguess where she was coming from and probably deciding that she was being awkward when she wasn't being awkward, she told herself mulishly.

Then he moved, levering himself upright, and she frowned furiously at the loaf of bread because she knew she wasn't only being awkward, she was almost fizzing with offended pride at his rejection before.

So if he had any sense he would keep his distance because if he dares to touch me now I'm likely to go for him with this knife!

He knew it too, the swine, because he hit so fast that he had the knife from her hand and put safely out of reach before she could even blink.

'OK.' He spun her round. 'Let's have this out.'

'Have what out?' She glared at his chest. The sweater he was wearing was made of the softest cashmere and she already knew how smooth and warm it felt to touch so she didn't need to fold her hands across her body to stop herself from finding out. 'I don't want to have anything out.'

'Well, I do,' he said. 'And I want to start by apologising for being a stiff-necked boor back there.'

Her shrug of indifference to his apology forced him to pull in a deep breath.

'I also apologise for misjudging you two years ago. I am sorry I read your letters and I'm sorry that I led you to believe I was marrying you for Rose's sake and to keep control of Salvatore stock.'

Her chin came up. 'Are you saying you didn't marry me for those reasons?'

He took in another of those breaths. 'I am saying I'm

sorry if I gave you that impression,' he persisted. 'And stop trying to turn this into another fight!'

'I'm not,' she denied while her blue eyes locked for battle.

He opened his mouth to answer, then closed it again when he took the mammoth decision not to take her on. 'Let's stick to the issues,' he gritted. 'What is important now is that we have two babies and your health to consider, which means we've got to stop fighting all the time and start to organise our lives to accommodate everyone's needs. So tomorrow we see a doctor and attempt to put all your fears at rest about your pregnancy. Then we are going to need somewhere else to live that is out of the city. Somewhere both you and Rose will breathe healthier air that will also be big enough to give us all our own bit of space. It is also important that we move quickly because Rose might be released from hospital next week and we are going to have to pull out all the stops to organise ourselves before that happens. We are going to need a full complement of staff—'

He was doing it again and playing the trouble-shooter, planning everything as if they were embarking on a new business project.

'You don't like servants littering up your house.' She tossed in a spanner.

'Do I have a choice?' he countered. 'You are pregnant and about to become a full-time mother, which has to take priority over my likes or dislikes.'

'Very good of you,' she commended.

'I wasn't trying to be a good boy, Shannon,' he sighed impatiently. 'I am trying to be practical. I would like to think *you* were going to be sensible and accept that you can't maintain a full-time career as well as everything else, but I don't hold out much hope of convincing you of that.'

'Too right,' she agreed. 'Is there anything else you've

decided about our future while you had this private meeting with yourself?'

She was still gunning for a war. Luca's eyes narrowed. He was just trying to decide whether to let her have war when the bell by the lift gave a short ring, announcing that their food had arrived.

Problem solved, he thought with relief as he swung away and strode out of the kitchen, wishing he knew where they were going from here because one thing was certain—they had resolved nothing and, if anything, become more entrenched in hostilities than they had been before.

He sanctioned the lift to come up, then stood sizzling in his own angry frustration while he waited for it to arrive. A waiter stood there holding a flat pizza box. Luca exchanged it for some money, then sent the lift doors sliding shut again. The owner of the restaurant must think he'd lost his head ordering pizza. If he'd been asked the question he would have given an affirmative by reply. He lost his head a long time ago to a red-haired witch with blue eyes and a nature that was more stubborn than his own!

He turned and strode back to the kitchen. Shannon had laid the table. He placed the pizza box down in the middle, then opened the lid. The moment she looked at it he could see she didn't want it. She just stood there by the table staring at it as if it were the worst offering he could have presented.

'What now?' he asked and his voice sounded husky, though he didn't know why it did.

'It's got cheese on it.'

'Pizza usually has cheese on it.'

'I forgot,' she murmured, then pressed her lips together and to his surprise they started to shake. 'I don't think I can have cheese. I don't think I can have eggs or milk or coffee or—anything in case it's bad for the baby!'

He was momentarily stunned. It had never occurred to

him that babies and certain foods did not go together. Was she right? Hell, what did he know? This was as new to him as it was to her.

She looked up at him then and his heart tilted. It was amazing how such a tough woman could turn into weak, vulnerable baby in a blink of an eye. 'No, don't cry,' he said and now his voice was sounding thick. 'Surely the odd slice of pizza cannot be dangerous?'

'I don't know. That's the point. I only asked for it to annoy you,' she admitted. 'But I did intend to eat it.'

'Idiota,' he sighed. 'Look, do you want me to order something else? I can have it here in—'

'No, I don't want anything else.' Then she really knocked him sideways when she ran sobbing from the kitchen, leaving him standing there feeling punch-drunk by the swing of emotions that had been taking place here tonight.

Shannon slammed into the bedroom and threw herself face down on the bed. She wished she knew what was wrong with her. She had never felt so messed up in her entire life! She wanted one thing, then she wanted the exact opposite. She wanted to keep hitting out at him and she wanted desperately to cling! It wasn't fair—none of it was fair.

The bed depressed as he came to lie down beside her. 'Stop it,' he said. 'Or you will make yourself sick again.'

'I'm frightened!' She punched the pillow by her head because she hated—*hated* feeling like this.

'I know.' He released a sigh and gathered her in.

'I'm so fed up with everything always going wrong for us, Luca! I thought we had it all sorted, now it's all gone haywire again and—'

'Now listen to me, you crazy little hellion,' he cut in fiercely, coming to loom over her so he could give her shoulders a gentle shake. 'Nothing is going to go wrong.

You are not your sister and you have got to stop thinking that you might be, do you hear?'

She looked at him through big, dark, make-me-believe-it, pleading eyes and— To hell with it, Luca thought, and gave in to what he had been aching to do all evening. He lowered his head, then crushed her trembling mouth. It took about two seconds after that for the sobs to start slowing. Another second later and she was kissing him back.

And if this wasn't worth fighting to hell and back for then life wasn't worth living at all, he thought as they both gave in to what they knew they should not be giving into until they'd consulted with a doctor. They made love with fire and passion. When it came time to join they did it with such gentle care and tenderness that it was a whole new mind-blowing experience on its own.

Afterwards they fell asleep in each other's arms while the pizza dried up in its box in the kitchen, and they awoke the next morning pretending they didn't feel guilty and worried that they'd tempted fate to spring yet another lousy deal on them with a doctor's report that sex was out for the next eight months, because both of them knew they'd struggle to stay the course.

CHAPTER TEN

FORTUNATELY the doctor said no such thing. He was very understanding of Shannon's fears and reassured her that her sister's problems had been a personal physical weakness and nothing genetically linked. She was fit and healthy. There was absolutely no reason why she shouldn't have a perfectly normal pregnancy and he told them to go away and get on with their marriage. 'Enjoy.' He grinned and wished them well as they left.

They were dazed—both of them. They'd become so used to bad luck dogging them that good news was difficult to accept.

The moment they were alone Luca pulled her into his arms and kissed her. 'I am off the hook,' he announced with feeling, and she laughed because she understood exactly what he meant because she felt the same way herself.

Rose was beautiful. Shannon couldn't believe the changes in the baby girl since she'd last seen her. She was all pink and cute with her mother's blue eyes and her father's silk dark hair. She cried as she held her. It was silly to cry because in reality she was so filled with love for this tiny, tiny sweet creature that she should have been laughing.

The nurse who was going to come with Rose when they left the hospital was called Maria. She was young and dark and so incredibly shy that she blushed every time Luca sent her a smile. He played on the shyness, being an utterly incorrigible Latin male. Then he would look at Shannon holding Rose and his expression would alter to a dark, dark, heavy-lashed density that would liquidise her insides. A teasing Latin male and a desiring Latin male were two different people: one was harmless, the other—wasn't.

When it was time for them to leave to go and visit a house Luca wanted to show her, it was Maria's arms that were waiting to take the baby.

Tension fizzed in the atmosphere as they drove out of Florence. It belonged to that old breathtaking excitement they'd used to share in those first few heady days and weeks before they'd become lovers, when their awareness of each other had been so needle-sharp it had been electric. This time it came from a new sharp sense of belonging. They were joined by the seed Luca had planted inside her and she was nurturing.

She was going to have Luca's child.

Her hand crept out to cover his where it moulded a squat racing gear stick. He didn't say a word but his fingers spread a little to gather hers in and the fizz had something physical to feed off as they drove on into the Tuscan countryside, passing through Fiesole on their way.

'This house isn't going to be another Salvatore Villa, is it?' Shannon quizzed dubiously.

'Wait and see.' Luca grinned, and it was one of those lazily teasing, natural white toothed grins that wrenched at her vulnerable heart.

Everything about her felt vulnerable today. She felt soft and serene and unbelievably female. It was the oddest sensation yet warm and nice. Until her meeting with the doctor she had been a worrying tumble of excitement and fear. She was still scared but now she felt joyful with it.

'You look so beautiful today,' Luca murmured huskily.

Could he see how she was feeling? She had to assume so because, even when they'd thought they'd hated each other, he had still been able to pick up on her every thought and emotion as if they belonged to him.

And maybe they did.

They pulled off a lane onto a clay driveway that took them through pastureland that gave way to the most perfect shallow valley with woodland and meadows and even a narrow stream.

Her first sighting of the house set her gasping. 'How did you find this?' she asked breathlessly.

'It belongs to me.' He sent her a wry smile. 'I was left it by my maternal grandfather.'

'Your mother used to live here?'

'Don't sound so shocked,' he mocked. 'She did not become a Salvatore until she married one,' he reminded her dryly. 'She was a Monteriggioni; they were wine growers,' he extended. 'They owned huge tracks of land around here and produced some of the best wine in Tuscany. When the wine industry had to modernise to keep up with New World wines, my grandfather decided he was too old for such radical change so he sold on the vineyards but kept the house and a large piece of surrounding land. As children we all loved to come and stay here because we were allowed a kind of freedom we could never be allowed in the centre of Florence.'

Shannon could understand why. This beautiful place was a haven to children.

Then there was the house.

Luca stopped the car, then sat back to give her a few minutes to absorb the two-storey frontage with rough stone walls, a clay roof and long, narrow windows with green shutters.

'How old is it?' she asked curiously.

'Fifteenth century, at a guess,' he said. 'The guessing part is because we could not trace it back further than the fifteenth century—which does not mean it was not here.'

Getting out of the car, he came round to open her door and help her to alight. Their hands linked again. He began drawing her towards a pair of solid-looking front doors.

Shannon was shocked to step through them then find herself standing in what she could only describe as country rustic. No grand display of priceless art collections. No exquisite renaissance furniture that made you want to stand and admire rather than use.

'It's amazing,' she murmured as they walked slowly from room to room of pure old-fashioned magic. The rough plastered walls were plain painted, the floors beneath her feet cool stone leading to wood then back to stone again. Every room was fully furnished and looked as if it hadn't been altered in centuries. 'I can't believe you never told me about this place.'

'It never came up in conversation.'

'Well, it should have done,' she chided. 'It's so wonderful.'

'Grazie,' he said. 'My grandparents left it to me because from being quite small I had apparently always claimed that this would be where I would live when I had a family.'

He was being gently mocking but she could hear the affection in his voice. 'And did you make that claim?' she asked.

'Sì,' he admitted. 'So now you know you have married a countryman at heart instead of an arrogant Florentine.'

Shannon turned to study him curiously. He was standing beside her dressed in one of his sharp business suits and looking about as glossy as a man of means could look. He should appear totally out of place here but oddly he didn't; she only had to superimpose a casually dressed Luca over the sharp-suited one to know he would look very at home.

'Then you're both,' she declared and wandered away to check out the next room, aware that his gaze was following her and aware that he'd read some kind of challenge in that remark.

Sexual challenge. It was all around them. Last night they had come together in a fever of passion they knew they should have resisted. Today all need to resist anything had been removed, so the passion shimmered like the sun coming in through the slats covering some of the windows.

They moved on through room after room arguing lightly over which wing would be a family wing and which would be reserved as work space. 'We could move in here today and not have to do a single thing to it,' she said eventually. 'Who has been keeping it this clean?'

'We used to have a housekeeper called Fantasia,' Luca said. 'She was here for so long I cannot recall a time when she wasn't.'

Shannon spun from the view she had been admiring through one of the windows. 'But she isn't here now?'

'Sadly no. She passed away a couple of years ago.' He walked off to straighten a painting that was hanging crooked on a wall.

'You were fond of her,' she probed.

'I adored her,' he sighed, standing back to check his handiwork. 'She ruled my life with a rod of iron and the best *osso buco* you could ever taste.'

'Impossible to replace, then.'

'Sì,' he agreed. 'So we won't even try. Instead we will have a very young, very modern team of staff to go with our very young and very modern family.' He swung round to face her suddenly. 'Do you want to take a look upstairs now?'

Oh, my, Shannon thought as desire coiled through the air like a magic love potion. She let him take her hand again to lead her up one of several staircases she'd noticed as they'd walked the ground floor.

They checked out bedroom after bedroom, found the nursery wing with just about everything a child could desire. It was like an enchanted place that had become lost in time. Everything was old and well used like the rest of the house, the only obviously updated features being the exquisite bathrooms—one attached to every room.

'Where are the staff?' she thought to ask as they stood in one of the larger bedrooms containing a huge four-poster bed that reached up to the high beamed ceiling.

'I gave them the day off so we could look around—uninterrupted.'

And Shannon swerved away from the heavy-lashed expression to pretend a deep interest in the handmade rug covering the richly polished floorboards beneath her shoes.

'Well...' she tried to take in some air by lifting her chin and turning full circle '...you will certainly have your own space here just as you wanted.'

'If that was a subtle hint for me to choose my own bedroom, then forget it. I sleep where you sleep.'

Her heart tripped a couple of beats.

'So take your pick,' he invited.

Her cheeks began to heat. Other parts of her began to join in. 'Some other time,' she said nervously and started backing away because he was most definitely stalking.

'But you look tired.'

'I do not,' she denied as the backs of her legs hit the edge of the bed and she knew she'd been carefully herded.

'You need to take regular rests. The good doctor said so.'

'Not for what you have in mind,' she derided. 'Don't you dare!' she protested when his hand lifted to tug at his tie.

But he did dare. Another stride and he was standing right in front of her. The tie came off, his jacket landed on the polished wood floor. She had a choice now, Shannon knew that. She could fight or she could surrender. His dark eyes flamed as he began undoing the buttons on his shirt. A deeply bronzed chest appeared with its covering of deliciously inviting dark hair.

Her eyelashes flickered in time with her accelerated heartbeat. The heat and the scent of him were going to her head.

'You planned to do this in this room, didn't you?' she murmured accusingly.

'Of course. It is the best room. Are you going to undress yourself or do you want me to do it?'

Still hovering between fight and surrender, she drew out the moment for a few long seconds. Then she relaxed her shoulders. 'This is your seduction, *caro*,' she murmured provocatively.

So he removed his clothes with a tantalising slowness. He teased her senses with hands that knew exactly where to touch. They made love into the afternoon and fell asleep together, as they did every night afterwards in that same bedroom with its big four poster bed and windows that overlooked the rolling Tuscan hills.

Rose came home. It was quite a shock to Shannon's system to find herself fully responsible for this precious little being who was so dependent on her for everything. But with Maria's help she managed. She learned to be a mother. It took weeks to feel really confident but she got there in the end.

She worked most mornings in her office. The afternoons were dedicated to Rose. Luca was busy—very busy. With Angelo gone he was having to do the work of two but breakfast time belonged strictly to Rose. And no matter how busy he was he still came home every night to share a meal with Shannon and, of course, the four-poster bed.

On the surface everything seemed absolutely perfect. Shannon was carrying her baby with an ease that surprised everyone. She was happy with her new life and it showed in the way she quite simply glowed. Luca's mother was so delighted to learn that they were moving into her old home that she was rarely away. She clung to Rose and, Shannon suspected, assuaged her grief for her lost son by pouring love into his baby daughter. Sophia became Shannon's mentor in everything to do with baby concerns. Renata still continued to hold herself aloof but as the months rolled on even she unbent and began to like her again.

Everything was pretty much perfect. Like the calm after a terrible storm, everyone seemed willing to work together to help make this new life they were building run as smoothly as it could. Shannon was happy. She felt healthy and alive and so enervated that nothing could bring her down. She even flew to London a couple of times during the early months to consult with clients. Though she did so in the pampered luxury of Luca's private jet with Rose and Maria along because she refused to be separated from her baby, and Fredo was there to drive her everywhere she needed to go.

She worked, she played, she made love with Luca. The only tiny, tiny cloud on her sunny horizon was that Luca had not once said he loved her. The look in his eyes told her he did but the words were never spoken, so she didn't say them either and just hoped that he could see in her eyes what she could see in his. One day we will feel safe enough to say it, she assured herself. I can be patient. Everything else is as perfect as it can be. She could feel her baby living inside her and had never felt so complete as a woman. She loved her house, her life, her family and it showed. She radiated contentment and happiness.

She forgot to be scared.

August arrived with a simmering heatwave. Florence heaved under its enormous weight. The streets throbbed with day-tripping tourists and those residents of Florence who could do moved out into the country or took their annual vacations simply to escape.

Even Luca decided to work from his office at the house rather than brave the hot, heaving flood in the city. Shannon was almost eight months pregnant and so incredibly beautiful it made his heart ache every time he looked at her. Rose had blossomed, developing an enchanting little personality of her own. She had recently discovered how to crawl and was causing minor mayhem wherever she was set loose.

She was doing so now, he observed with a grin as he lounged in the terrace doorway looking out towards the garden. He'd just changed out of casual shorts and a loose tee shirt into a suit because he had a meeting to attend in Florence, which meant braving the gridlock that clogged up the city in heat that seared. He did not want to go. He wanted to stay right here and watch the baby girl fight for her freedom while Shannon, looking amazing in a fitted white shift that moulded the heavily pregnant shape, held firm to the straps of Rose's little white dungarees.

They were supposed to be sitting quietly beneath the shade of a sun umbrella but Rose had different ideas. She'd spotted one of the resident cats and was determined to chase it.

'No, Rose, no,' Shannon said firmly. 'The sun is too hot, you must—'

The baby broke loose. Luca was still trying to work out how Shannon had allowed it to happen when he saw her lunge forward in an effort to catch Rose again. Then the lunge suddenly changed into something else entirely. He saw her freeze like a statue for a second, then her cry hit his eardrums as her face contorted and she slumped to the grass in a ball of pain.

His heart punched a hole in his throat as he launched himself into movement. He ran across the terrace and onto the grass to fall to his knees beside her and placed a hand on the rounded curve of her spine.

'What happened—what?' he demanded sharply.

'Pain,' she gasped and even as she said it the next agonised spasm shot through her, forcing the breath from her throat on a sharp, keening cry.

The sound pierced the heat-laden sunlit air like the bay

of a wounded animal. Dropping down even lower he curved his arms right around her as her fingers pawed desperately at the ground. *'Cara,'* he kept saying, *'cara,'* because he did not know what to do and she was so paralysed by the pain.

He must have called for help though he did not recall doing it. People came running from all directions. Someone scooped up the escaping Rose, another yelled for Maria. The nurse came at a run and joined him on her knees beside Shannon, who was heaving in air then not breathing at all as her whole body locked inside a soul-raking, thick, extended moan.

'What's happening—what's happening?' she gasped out a few seconds later. 'This can't be right, can it?'

'Your baby has decided to arrive early and is in a great hurry,' Maria said. 'We need to get you to the hospital very quickly, *signora*.' Then she looked at Luca with urgent dark eyes and added, 'Very quickly, *signor*,' and Luca felt his blood run cold.

Then the next paroxysm caught hold of Shannon and he was plunging himself into incisive efficiency, making decisions and snapping out orders as he climbed to his feet with Shannon in his arms.

'Luca,' she sobbed. 'I'm frightened.'

'Shh,' he soothed through teeth locked by tension. 'Everything is going to be fine.'

He began striding towards the house with Shannon's fingers clutching at his neck and Maria running along beside him while countless other people scattered like flies. Fredo was waiting in the outer courtyard with the rear door to the Mercedes open and his face drawn with concern.

'The local hospital, *signor*,' Maria advised gravely.

'Get going!' he rasped even as he got in the rear seat of the car with Shannon.

Fredo leapt up then raced around the bonnet. The car took

off down the drive like a bullet kicking up red clay dust as it went. Shannon's fingernails were scoring crescents into the side of Luca's neck and those God-awful breath-locking groans were filling the car.

The contraction eased, leaving Shannon weak and trembling. Her fingernails eased their grip on his neck. Then she rolled her head against his arm and opened her eyes to look at him. It was like looking into hell.

'It's the same,' she whispered and he knew she was talking about Keira.

'It is not the same,' he bit out sternly. 'It is happening a few weeks early, that is all. Have you not got enough to do here without scaring yourself too?'

Her eyes clung to the ferocity of his expression, drawing strength from it as the next pain hit. This time there was no let-up. Fredo drove like a maniac. They hit gridlock on the outskirts of Fiesole. Fredo sat on the horn until cars and coaches began reluctantly edging out of their way. A traffic policeman on a motorbike suddenly appeared beside them. Fredo spoke to him, and the guy only had to glance into the rear of the car and a second later he was cutting them a corridor through the traffic with Fredo riding on his back wheel.

They arrived at the hospital entrance to a waiting team of medics. The moment Luca climbed out of the car with his burden they were swooping down on them. They wanted to place her on a trolley but Shannon wouldn't let go of him. Luca had to be tough with himself and lower her down there with her fingernails still clutching his neck with enough force to draw blood.

What followed became a mind-locking blur of swinging doors and medics throwing questions at him that he tried to answer without biting off their heads. Shannon had a tight grip on one of his hands now and was not going to let go, forcing the medical team to work round him.

Eventually someone found him a chair and suggested that he sit down. He did so without relinquishing his grasp on Shannon's hand and leant closer so he could curve an arm across the crown of her head as if he was trying to protect her from all of this.

'It is going to be OK,' he whispered fiercely. 'Very healthy babies are born at thirty-five weeks.'

She nodded. 'We have Rose as living proof.'

He nodded too and held her frightened gaze while trying hard not to recall all of Keira's tragedies before Rose. From then on everything happened so quickly it threw everyone into a panic as the baby arrived with a speed that took everyone by surprise.

'You have a son,' the attending doctor announced, then there was a scurry of activity, 'Do not be alarmed that you cannot hear him cry. My team are working on that; give them a few seconds.'

But those few seconds felt like a lifetime. Luca held Shannon's gaze and counted those seconds with each throbbing drumbeat of his heart. Shannon was so still he knew she was doing the same thing while all around them everyone else got on with their tasks as if it were nothing unusual for them to deliver five-week premature babies for parents with a family history of tragic premature births.

Then it came—that first weak little cry that wound its way around everyone. Shannon released a single strangled sob of relief and Luca had to close his eyes while he fought a hard battle with control.

Then another cry came—and another. 'You have a fighter,' someone remarked. 'This little man is going to be fine…'

Luca paced the corridor outside Shannon's room and tried to come to terms with the miracle he had just witnessed. Why did women willingly put themselves through it? Why did men cling to the belief that they had the right to make it happen at all?

A nurse came out of Shannon's room. 'You can go back in now.' She smiled.

He shot through the door like a bullet to find Shannon reclining against a bank of pillows and looking calm and serene and so achingly beautiful that he did not hesitate. Making directly for the bed, he sat down on it and looked deeply into her soft blue eyes.

'I love you,' he said, then fastened his mouth on hers in the gentlest kiss meant to seal that declaration. 'I wanted you to know that before we exchanged another word,' he explained as soon as he broke contact. 'I should have said it months ago but I did not think it would mean anything after—'

Shannon's fingers came up to cover his lips, and she smiled a tender smile. 'Just say it again,' she instructed softly.

He heaved in a tense breath and caught her fingers, passion glowing from dark, dark eyes. 'I love you—*ti amo*,' he repeated huskily. 'Always—*sempre e per sempre*.' He kissed her fingertips and watched her eyes begin to mist with happy tears. 'You are my life—*lei è la mia vita*. My soul—*la mia anima*.'

Shannon couldn't stop the small chuckle. 'You don't have to repeat everything twice.'

'Yes, I do,' he stated fiercely. 'I owe these words to you. I owe you for every single day I have let pass by without telling you how much you mean to me.'

'I never said them to you,' she pointed out candidly.

'You had no need to say anything. You married me knowing what I believed, that was enough.'

'And you married me believing what you thought you knew,' she countered. 'Does this mean I have to say the words back to you for you to know I feel the same way about you?'

'Sì,' A hint of his old arrogance appeared. 'What man lays his heart bare without expecting his love to do the same for him?'

'Idiota.' She laughed softly and twisted her fingers free so she could wind her arms around his neck. 'I love you,' she whispered. 'I always have and I always will—even though you are a fraud,' she informed him teasingly. 'You decided that today was a good day to tell me because I gave you a beautiful son and you're so full up with love and pride you don't know what to do with it.'

'Ah, well…' He sent her a lazy grin. 'There is that too, I suppose.' Then immediately he was serious. 'We are never doing this again,' he announced huskily. 'That a woman in the twenty-first century should have to go through so much to give birth is barbaric.'

'Primitive acts of untrammelled lust bring forth primitive results,' Shannon countered. Then she frowned. 'Why are you staring at me like that? I wasn't that awful, was I?'

'You were amazing.' He took her face between his hands and kissed her again—with fierce passion this time. 'You were strong and courageous and I was a useless waste of time and space. I—'

'You held my hand and kissed me all the way through,' Shannon reminded him gently. 'You kept me strong, Luca.'

'We are still never doing this again,' he maintained. 'I married you to love and cherish, not to force you to be strong!'

'Where is my son?' she fretted suddenly. 'When they took him away they said they would only be gone a few minutes. That was—'

'Be at peace. He is in safe hands.' He soothed her with the gentle caress of his fingers to her cheek. 'My mother has him.' He grinned then.

'Your mother is here?' Shannon widened her eyes in surprise.

'Sophia and Renata too.' He nodded. 'The last I saw of them they were trying to decide if he looked Irish or Florentine.'

'Oh, goodness me!' Shannon gasped in horror. 'He hasn't grown red hair since I last saw him, has he?'

'No, it is still as dark as mine.' Luca laughed. Then suddenly wasn't laughing. 'He is beautiful. *You* are beautiful. I adore red hair. I adore you. And when I get you home again I will enjoy showing you how much I adore you.'

'You're talking sex already,' Shannom sighed out chidingly.

'I am talking *love*,' Luca corrected and set about showing her the difference.